'Beautiful and devastating' *Washington Post*

'Near perfect . . . a study in classic supernatural fiction, told with a skill that we enjoy for its own sake'
Independent

'Stark, layered, ominous and yet appealing . . . Mr. Joyce delivers relief along with satisfaction and wonder'
New York Times

'You'll laugh, albeit nervously; you'll cry, unless you're completely heartless; you'll give your nearest and dearest hugs without really being able to explain why you're so glad to see them – really, what more do you want from a novel?' *SFX*

The Silent Land

Graham Joyce

Copyright © Graham Joyce 2010
All rights reserved

The right of Graham Joyce to be identified as the author
of this work has been asserted by him in accordance with the
Copyright, Designs and Patents Act 1988.

First published in Great Britain in 2010 by
Gollancz
An imprint of the Orion Publishing Group
Orion House, 5 Upper St Martin's Lane,
London WC2H 9EA
An Hachette UK Company

This edition published in Great Britain in 2011 by Gollancz

1 3 5 7 9 10 8 6 4 2

A CIP catalogue record for this book
is available from the British Library

ISBN 978 0 575 08387 5

Typeset by Deltatype Ltd, Birkenhead, Merseyside

Printed and bound by CPI Group (UK) Ltd, Croydon, CR0 4YY

The Orion Publishing Group's policy is to use papers that are natural,
renewable and recyclable products and made from wood grown in
sustainable forests. The logging and manufacturing processes are expected
to conform to the environmental regulations of the country of origin.

www.grahamjoyce.net

www.orionbooks.co.uk

To Sue, rescuer

Remember me when I am gone away,
Gone far away into the silent land;
When you can no more hold me by the hand,
Nor I half turn to go, yet turning stay.
Remember me when no more day by day
You tell me of our future that you plann'd:
Only remember me; you understand
It will be late to counsel then or pray.
Yet if you should forget me for a while
And afterwards remember, do not grieve:
For if the darkness and corruption leave
A vestige of the thoughts that once I had,
Better by far you should forget and smile
Than that you should remember and be sad.

Remember, Christina Rossetti

It was snowing again. Gentle six-pointed flakes from a picture book, settling on her jacket sleeve. The mountain air prickled with ice and the savour of pine resin. Zoe pulled the air into her lungs, feeling the cracking cold of it before letting go. And when the mountain horn seemed to nod and sigh back at her, she almost thought she could die in that place, and happily.

If there are few moments in life that come as clear and as pure as ice, when the mountain breathed back at her, Zoe knew that she had trapped one such moment and that it could never be taken away. Everywhere was snow and silence. Snow and silence; the complete arrest of life; a rehearsal and a pre-echo of death.

But her breath was warm and it said no to that. She pointed her skis down the hill. They looked like weird talons of brilliant red and gold in the powder snow as she waited, ready to swoop. *I am alive. I am an eagle.* Several hundred metres below lay the dark outline of Saint-Bernard-en-Haut, their Pyrenean resort village; across to the west, the irregular humps and horns of the mountain range. The sun was up now; in a few minutes there would be more skiers to break the eerie morning spell. But right now they had the powder and the morning entirely to themselves.

There was a whisper behind her. It was the effortless

track of Jake's skis as he came over the ridge and caught up with her.

He cruised to an elegant stop beside her. In contrast to her fashionable ski suit of lilac and white he wore black, and the morning sun burst on his bulbous black sunglasses in an iridescent flare. He stood still, sharing the moment with her. She fancied she could see his breath rising from him like a faint oyster-coloured mist. He took off his sunglasses and blinked back at her. Jake had close-cropped black hair and baby-blue peepers that she'd fallen in love with instantly, even if his large ears had taken her a little longer. A single, enormous snowflake floated onto his eyelashes.

Jake fractured the silence with a whoop of pure pleasure. 'Whooo-hooooo!!!!' He held his ski poles aloft and offered his dancing arse to the mountain. The sound of his shriek echoed around the crags, a celebration and a violation of nature all at the same time.

'You shouldn't do that. You don't show the mountain your arsehole, arsehole,' Zoe said.

'Why not, arsehole?'

'I don't know why, arsehole. I just said it.'

'Couldn't help myself. This is perfection.'

It was. It was flawless. Immaculate, shrink-wrapped perfection on sticks.

'You ready to go?' she asked.

'Yep. Let's do it.'

Zoe was the more accomplished skier of the two. Jake could be faster, but in a reckless way, skiing right at the razor edge of his ability. She could always thrash him over a distance. To ski down to the village without a pause would take fifteen minutes. An hour and a half to get up on the combination of chair- and drag lifts, and fifteen minutes to get down. They'd got up early to beat the holiday-making hordes for this first run of the morning. Because this – the tranquillity, the silence, the undisturbed powder and the eerie feeling of proximity to an eagle's flight – was what it was all about.

Jake hit the west side of the steep but broad slope and she took the east, carving matching parallel tracks through the fresh snow. Her skis whispered to the powder in thrilling intimacy as she plunged down the slope. Just the sound coming from her own skis was like having some creature or supernatural being racing behind her, trying to speak a story into her ear.

But at the edge of the slope, near the curtain of trees, she felt a small slab of snow slip from underneath her. It was like she'd been bucked, so she took the fall-line to recover her balance. Before she'd dropped three hundred metres the whisper of her skis was displaced by a rumble.

Zoe saw at the periphery of her vision that Jake had come to a halt at the side of the piste and was looking back up the slope. Irritated by the false start they'd made, she etched a few turns before skidding to a halt and turning to look back at her husband. The rumble became louder. There was a pillar of what looked like grey smoke unfurling in silky banners at the head of the slope, like the heraldry of snow armies. It was beautiful. It made her smile.

Then her smile iced over. Jake was speeding straight towards her like a dart. His face was rubberised and he mouthed something as he flew at her.

'Get to the side! To the side!'

She knew now that it was an avalanche. Jake slowed,

batting at her with his ski pole. 'Get into the trees! Hang on to a tree!'

The rumbling had become a roaring in her ears, drowning Jake's words. She pushed herself down the fall-line, scrambling for traction, trying to accelerate away from the roaring cloud breaking behind her like a tsunami at sea. Jagged black cracks appeared in the snow in front of her. She angled her skis towards the side of the slope, heading for the trees, but it was too late. She saw Jake's black suit go bundling past her like clothes in a laundrette as he was turned by the great mass of smoke and snow. Then she too was punched off her feet and carried through the air, twisting, spinning, turning in the white-out. She remembered something about spreading her arms around her head. For a few moments it was like being agitated inside a washing machine, turned head over heels a few times, until at last she was dumped heavily in a rib-cracking fall. Then there came a chattering noise, like the amplified jaws of a million termites chewing on wood. The noise itself filled her ears and muffled everything, and then there was silence, and the total whiteness faded to grey, and then to black.

Total silence, total darkness.

She tried to move but couldn't. Then she felt herself choking, because her mouth and her nostrils were packed with snow. She hawked some snow out of her throat. She felt the snow trickling cold at the back of her nasal passage. She coughed again and was able to gasp a lungful of air.

If she had expected to come round in the whiteness of snow, everything was black. She could breathe, but could barely move. She flexed her fingers inside her leather ski gauntlets. There was micro-movement. She sensed her hands were locked in position about twenty or thirty centimetres in front of her face. Her fingers were splayed wide inside the gauntlets. She tried to wriggle her fingers but nothing would move beyond that micro-flexing inside the glove. She stuck out her tongue and felt cold air.

She heaved her body with no result; and instantly descended into a panic in which she was hyperventilating and feeling the booming of her own heart. Then it occurred to her that she might have only a pocket of trapped air to depend on, and so she slowed her breathing right down. She told herself to be calm.

You're in a snow tomb, be calm.

She breathed gently. Her heart stopped banging.

A snow tomb? You think that's good?

There was almost a split inside herself as the part of her that wanted to give in to panic made an argument with the side of her that knew if she wanted to survive she should stay composed.

Are you calm now? Are you? Are you? Right, when you are calm, call for your husband. He will come.

'Jake!'

She shouted his name, twice. Her voice sounded alien, distant, muffled, like something down a poor telephone line. She figured that her ears were plugged tight with snow.

She flexed her fingers again and still nothing gave way. She tried every joint, like a warm-up exercise in the gymnasium, starting with her toes, moving on to her ankles and her knees, hips, elbows, shoulders. There was no relief. The snow had packed her hard.

There was a tiny movement at her neck. That and the clearway around her mouth made her think that her instinct to fold her arms in front of her face had saved her thus far. She figured that she'd made an air pocket.

Call him again. He will come.

'Jake!'

You're going to die. In a snow tomb.

She didn't even know which country she was going to die in. They were right on the mountain border between France and Spain and the local people spoke a language that belonged to neither. She remembered that the Pyrenees were named for a tomb by the Ancient Greeks.

No, you're not in a tomb. You're going to get out. Call him again.

Instead of calling again she tried to move the fingers of her left hand, one by one. Her thumb and forefinger were paralysed, as was her middle finger, but as she pressed with her ring finger she sensed a minute crumbling and a tiny movement in one fingertip. Something infinitesimal gave way, and she was able to retract her finger perhaps a centimetre. The movement was matched by a strontium flare at the back of her retinas. Then a rainbow of sparks. Then blackness again.

But the message of tiny movement flew from the nerves in her finger to quicken her heartbeat.

Calm. Calm.

She continued to work her ring finger and after a while she found she could move it against her middle finger in a scissor-motion. She exercised this scissor movement between her wedding finger and her middle finger. *That's right; you're cutting your way out. Snip snip snip. Good girl. Cutting yourself free.*

She had no idea how long she would be able to breathe; how much air she had. She tried to be economical with her breathing, keeping it shallow, sipping at the air. Her head was banging with pain.

She continued to try to scissor away at the snow around her fingers until the muscles in her fingers cramped. She rested them, flexed them and began again. *Snip snip snip. Good girl.*

And with no prospect of movement something suddenly fell away and her other fingers became free, until she was able to flex all of them, back and forth. Then she felt her moving fingers brushing the side of her face.

Now she made tiny karate-chopping motions with the upper extent of her now flexible fingers, trying to find her other hand, hoping it had also come to rest close to her face. She was able to extend into and retract from the small space she had made. At last the free hand made contact with the other. She worked away until she was able to lay the palm of her free gauntlet over the back of the other. Then she pushed back into the snow, full force. Her first guess had been about right. She'd cradled a small pocket of air in front of her. She still had no idea how long this air would last. A minute? Three minutes? Ten minutes?

Don't think about that. Good girl.

She tried to wriggle her hand out of the gauntlet, knowing her fingernails would make the best tools for scraping her way out. But the gauntlets were strapped tight at the wrist to prevent the ingress of snow. In the immovable dark she tried to loosen the wrist strap of her right gauntlet, but the gauntleted fingers weren't sensitive enough to allow her to grab the strap.

Perhaps Jake would come. Unless he too was trapped.

Perhaps someone else would come. Perhaps they had helicopters circling overhead even as she thought these things. But no one else had been on the slope. It was likely that if the avalanche had been quite small no one would even know that it had happened.

Tomb. Greeks. Pyre means fire. You know. You know. Pyrenees. Shut up shut up.

'Jake!'

Her voice sounded a little louder in her own ears this time; but it also sounded helpless.

She tried again to grab at her wrist strap in the blackness. She heard the sound of Velcro parting, and the strap loosened. Grabbing the tip of her right gauntlet with her left hand she managed to inch it off. There was nowhere for the gauntlet to go: the thing was scratching her face, but she released it anyway and began to scrape with her fingernails at the snow just above her head.

Her breathing was coming shorter now. She was scratching at the packed snow but making no progress. The snow came free but didn't move. It had nowhere to go. She scratched harder.

She coughed again. There was something trickling at the back of her throat, making her cough. Then she stopped scratching and focused on the trickling. The fluid, the melted snow or saliva or whatever it was, was running from her nose into her throat. Instead of snot falling from her nose it was running backwards.

You are upside down.

She knew now with absolute certainty that she had been buried upside down, and vertically. Her feet were nearest to the surface of the snow, not her head. This meant that by scratching on the snow she'd been digging down, deeper into the snow, not up and out. That was why the snow wasn't flaking free. She'd been digging the wrong way.

She tried flexing her toe inside her boot. It moved a fraction, but the snow around her leg was too hard-packed to let her move her leg. She inched her ungloved hand to her neck and found she could reach her hand through the snow to her chest. By scratching she could push her hand to her hip, and the snow fell in clumps towards her face. Then her hand hit a solid object.

It was her ski pole.

The handle of the ski pole rested at hip height. She grabbed it and discovered it lay exactly in line with her thigh. At first it wouldn't move but by making a gentle sawing motion she could release a trickle of snow above her.

Saw it. That's right. Saw saw saw. Good girl. Saw your way out of this coffin.

Her arm cramped and her muscles spasmed, but she kept up the tiny incremental sawing motion. With mounting excitement she felt the pole jag on her ski boot. Almost hyperventilating again, she sawed the pole back and forth, and felt a tiny pop as the pole broke the surface of the snow. A pencil beam of brilliant sunlight penetrated her tomb as the pole acted like a conduit for electricity. Something indeterminate between a laugh and a cry bubbled from her lips. Her lungs sucked in the icy air and a sob erupted from her.

'Jake! Anyone! Help!'

She continued to saw away with her pole, trying to widen the narrow shaft to suck in some air, some sunshine, some life. But the effort exhausted her. When she stopped sawing all she could hear was her own ventilating lungs, a scratchy, underwater sound. Now her arm was cramping badly. She tried to ease it, but the ski pole twisted and the plastic basket at the end of it only dragged snow down into the aperture she'd made, closing off the pencil beam of light all over again.

She hung immobile, trying to steady her breathing, but she felt the pocket of air warming and thinning all over again. She felt dizzy. She felt her breathing drop through the gears and then a terrible surrender passed over her as she felt her consciousness shutting down.

Dimly from somewhere she heard a faint sound, like that of fingers sifting flour in a bowl. It was far off. Then it became a scratching, nearer.

And then she heard him.

'Zoe! I'm here! I'm here!'

'Oh God oh God oh God oh God!'

'I'm here. It's all right.'

She couldn't see him, but his voice was like light through a stained-glass window in a cathedral. She could feel him digging frantically around her boot. She could hear his panting and gasps of exertion

'It's no good, I'm going to have to get someone!' she heard him shout.

'No, Jake! Dig me out! Dig me out now! Don't leave! Don't!'

There was silence.

'Okay. I'm digging you out.'

'Work on one side.'

'What?'

'One side!'

'I can't hear you. I'm digging you out.'

*

It took Jake an hour to dig Zoe free of the snow. No one came by. First he dug her right leg free and then cleared a deep shaft down to her head, so that she was out of danger of suffocation even if she still couldn't move. Then at last he freed her arm and she was able to help him.

He barely had the strength to hoist her out of the snow-hole when she was clear. But together they got her out.

On their knees, they hugged for a long time; almost hugging the life out of each other.

'Look at your eyes!' she said. 'They're completely bloodshot!'

'The snow walloped me in the face.' He looked up and down the slope. 'When you want the piste to be teeming with people there's not a bastard in sight. Do you want to wait here while I go get someone?'

'I don't want to be left here, Jake.'

'Can you ski down?'

'No, I lost my skis. They're somewhere under the snow.'

'Mine too. We'll have to walk down to the next lift station. I'm frozen. I need to move to get warm. Are you up to it?'

'I feel okay. Really. Maybe it's the adrenalin, but I feel okay. Come on, let's go.'

They put their arms around each other and, trudging along the edge of the slope, they made slow progress down the mountain. Alive. Alive.

With light snow still falling around them it took maybe three-quarters of an hour of struggling through the deep snow in their heavy ski boots before they saw the overhead cables of a drag lift, with an intermediate station cabin about three hundred metres down the slope. The drag lift had been stopped. Neither was there any sign of activity on the slopes above or below them.

Zoe was shivering. Jake talked, mostly just to distract her. He told her that the trees had saved him. He'd been thrown against a slender pine and had flung his arms around it, swimming up its trunk as the snow deepened under him. Zoe grinned at him and nodded as he chattered about their escape. She recognised that he was in a state of shock. She knew that when they reached the drag-lift cabin the operator would radio for first-aiders and they would soon be whisked off the mountain.

But when they reached the cabin, it was empty. Through the smeared glass they could see one red and two green electronic lights shining under a row of switches on a console. The engines to turn the drag had been powered down. The glass door to the cabin stood very slightly ajar and heat was coming from inside. Jake pushed open the door.

'Come on, darlin' girl. We need to get you warm.'

'You think they shut down the mountain?'

'Likely. They maybe saw the avalanche and sent everyone down. Let's just sit here a while until you get some warmth back in your body.'

There was a seat with torn leather upholstery, and Zoe slumped into it. Jake had a quick look around the cabin.

'Hey!' She'd found a hip flask on the desk by the console.

'Gimme that!' Jake grabbed it, twisted open the cap and took a slug from the flask.

'Don't snatch! What's in it?'

'Dunno. It's fuck-awful. Have some.'

Zoe sniffed it, and took a slug herself. 'They won't mind. Look – here's some chocolate. I'm gonna munch it. Want some?'

'Naw, just give me the flask.'

There was a ski coat hanging behind the door with a rolled-up newspaper in the pocket. Two wide shovels and a snow brush leaned against one wall of the cabin. Though the engines were powered down, the glowing lights suggested the machinery all seemed to be switched on. An old-style walkie-talkie radio receiver hung from a peg. Jake took it down and flicked the switches. He got the sound of static but nothing else. He tried speaking into it a few times, but was only rewarded by more static. There was not much else in the grimy cabin, but at least it was warm. Outside the snow had started to come down heavier. They decided to sit and wait until someone came.

Jake took another swig from the hip flask, wincing. 'That was close,' he said. 'Close.'

'Very close. Too close.'

'We were lucky to walk away.'

Zoe looked at her husband and said, 'You know what? We're just a snowflake on God's eyelash. That's all we are.'

'What? If you're getting God just because you survived an avalanche I'm divorcing you on religious grounds.'

'Can I have another hug?'

'Come here. Have two. Have three. You can have all the bloody hugs you want.'

*

An hour later, still no one had turned up at the cabin. They finished what was in the hip flask and polished off the chocolate. They tried the walkie-talkie again but heard only the same static on the airwaves. Jake started flicking switches on the console, and with a great rumble and whistle of turbines, the engines powered up and the big wheel overhead started turning.

'Shut it down!' Zoe shouted.

'Why?'

'I dunno! Just shut it down! You don't know what you're doing!'

Jake shut the machinery down. 'Come on, we're going to have to walk all the way down the mountain.'

'Are you up to it?'

'I don't want to sit around here any more.'

They zipped up their coats and pulled on their hats and their gauntlets, and prepared to trudge down the mountain. Then Zoe noticed a set of skis leaning outside the cabin.

'Do you think we can take them? I mean, does that mean someone is still up here?'

'I dunno. Do they look like they've been used this morning?'

She inspected the skis. The fresh snow had fallen on them. 'No way of telling. Listen – I just had a bad thought. You don't suppose the lift operator was caught in the avalanche, do you?'

'What? In his cabin?'

'No. I mean, say, he was out inspecting the slopes. I don't know what they do exactly, but say he was on the slope, shovelling snow or inspecting the drag lift or something, and he got caught, like we did.'

'But they'd know. They'd be here. Looking for him.'

'You think?'

'Yeah. They're in radio contact all the time. In case of problems. They've shut the whole mountain down and he's gone. And no one is coming back until they open up the mountain again. Which may be tomorrow.'

'So why are the skis here?'

'Maybe they leave a spare set here all the time.'

'You don't suppose there's someone, you know, lying under the snow, do you?'

Jake tugged at an earlobe. 'Be realistic. If there is, he's dead. We've been here nearly two hours now.'

'We should make sure,' Zoe said. 'We should help if we can. We have to do everything we can.'

Jake nodded. 'Right. Right. Listen, this is what I want to do. I'm gonna put the skis on. This is a short lift. I'll take the drag to the top. If he's around, if he was out doing maintenance, he'll be somewhere close to the track of the drag.'

'You think it's a waste of time?'

'We couldn't live with ourselves if we didn't try. He might be lying there injured.'

Zoe took her lavender wool hat and put it on again. 'Okay. I'll come with you.'

'No. You're exhausted. And it will be quicker for me on skis.'

'I want to come.'

'Zoe, I don't mind telling you, you look terrible. Your eyes are red bloodshot, too. I didn't want to upset you. Maybe it was the pressure of the snow. But you look shaky. I'll just satisfy myself that there's no one lying on the track. If he's underneath the snow, there's nothing I can do anyway. Okay?'

Zoe blinked. They knew each other well enough.

They both had a strong sense of the right thing to do, and she knew Jake would go ahead and do it.

Jake kept a small screwdriver in his bumbag for adjusting the bindings on their skis and he was already employing it to adapt the found skis to fit his boots.

Jake hit some switches until the machinery started up again and the steel wheel overhead began rotating. Zoe went outside to where the T-bars were stacked up on the drag loop and tugged one of the poles around, waiting for him to shuffle into place. She handed him the T-bar and he took it without a word. Suddenly she didn't want him to leave her. She watched as the lonely drag pulled him up the slope and out of sight. It was still snowing. She went back inside the cabin.

The cabin was warm but she was shaking. She tried to close her eyes but when she did so violent images of the immediate impact of the avalanche came at her like hissing snakes. She felt her stomach squeeze.

Very soon she wished she hadn't allowed Jake to go out. It occurred to her that there could easily be a fresh avalanche. She got up and looked out through the dirty window of the cabin. Then she sat down again.

Jake was gone a long time. She felt hot. She pressed her hand to her brow, wondering if she had a fever. A sob broke out of her, completely unexpected. She got up and went to the window again, but all she could see was the vast whiteness of the mountain and the snow-bearing trees. She strained her ears to listen. There was nothing. The world out there was silent. The cabin felt tiny and vulnerable.

She'd almost fallen into a doze when a grey shape loomed outside the window. It was Jake, stepping out of his bindings. He came into the warmth of the cabin stamping his boots and shaking his head.

'Nothing at all?'

'I had a good check round at every pylon. If there is someone there, he's deep under the snow.'

'That's a creepy thought.' Zoe started crying.

Jake put his arm around her and kissed her. 'Hush up,' he said. 'Hush. You don't know there's anyone there! It was just an outside chance.'

'I know. Let me cry. I'm crying for us. It could have been us. It's the relief.' She sniffed and wiped her nose with the back of her gauntlet.

'Listen,' Jake said, after a few moments just holding her, 'I've had one of my great ideas. We can get down on the skis. There is a way.'

'On one set of skis?'

'You stand on the back of the skis and hold me around the waist. We make really slow traverses across the slope. We might fall over a few times but it's better than trying to walk through the snow. Honestly, it comes up to your balls in places.'

That's what they did. It was slow skiing, but it wasn't too difficult and it got them down. The entire slope, all the way, was empty of people and it was clear that the mountain authorities had evacuated and closed the slopes because of further avalanche risk.

They could see their hotel directly ahead of them. Even though it was only a little past midday, all the lights were on. It looked cosy, and inviting, and safe.

'I'm going to have a hot bath,' said Zoe.

'Yeah, you stink.'

'Thanks. And a sauna, cos I'm chilled to the bone. But you're not getting in with me.'

'And a glass of wine. Red.'

'And a steak. Rare.'

'Oozing with blood. And with mustard.'

'And ice cream.'

'What, on the steak?'

'And we're going to drink the bar dry.'

'Come on. Let me take these skis off. We can walk from here.'

2

The Hotel Varka nestled at the foot of the mountain, some distance from the centre of the village of Saint-Bernard-en-Haut but close to the nursery slopes. It boasted 'doorstep' skiing, which was true if shuffling along the flat valley floor for a couple of hundred metres can be considered skiing. The hotel offered four-star service, two bars (one with piano), a restaurant, a spa with sauna, ski shuttle and Wi-Fi Internet. It was more expensive than the Bennetts could normally afford, but this was a special holiday. They hadn't been skiing for a few years – and it was on the ski slopes at Chamonix that they'd originally met and fallen in love – so they'd rewarded themselves with this upgraded vacation.

With no respect for the notion of special holidays, the avalanche with its ferocious white teeth had snapped at their heels on only their second day.

The reception of the hotel was entered through electronically operated glass doors that hummed at their approach and opened with painful slowness. The lobby itself was dominated by a giant and perhaps overstated Christmas tree. It was beautifully illuminated by delicate blue lights, twinkling amid the branches like hovering sprites. Zoe and Jake made straight for the reception desk, wanting to let someone know about their ordeal, but for the moment the desk was deserted. They turned instead to the lift and rode it up the third floor, where they had their room.

Zoe immediately ran a hot bath and while it was filling she stripped off her ski gear. Jake collapsed on the bed, his arms flung back. Zoe kneeled beside him in her thermal underwear.

'You okay?'

'I am, actually,' he said. 'I feel okay.'

'We'll have to get some eye-drops. You look like a bloody zombie. We should get you checked out.'

'I don't need checking out. You're blood-shot and you're the one who got buried. You need checking out to make sure you're not whatsit. Traumatised.'

'What are they going to do? Give me counselling? Hold my hand? I'm fine, I don't need checking out. Some snow fell on me and I crawled out. End of story. What about you?'

'I feel fine. The only thing different is I feel ridiculously horny. Feel this.'

'Get off. Let me have my bath first.'

'Do you think it's like when people feel horny at funerals? Do you think it's the swish of the scythe? Makes you want to rut? Come here, *ma biche*.'

'Get off me, I'm chilled to the bone, Jake. You must be, too. Let me get in the bath first.'

Jake snatched up the phone. 'I'm going to tell some fucker what happened.'

'What do you think they're going to do? Don't you dare get a doctor for me! Come on, get in the bath with me. I don't want no doctor shining lights in my eyes. Come on. Afterwards you can do what you want to me.'

So Jake stripped off his ski gear and squeezed into

the hot bath along with Zoe, groaning and sighing. They sat face to face in the steam, hugging each other's knees, letting the heat penetrate and dissolve the chill in their bones.

They sat in silence. With his head resting on Zoe's knee, Jake seemed to drift off to sleep. At last the water started to cool around them so she shifted him, got out of the bath and wrapped a towel around her. Thinking that maybe she really should at least report their escape to someone, Zoe called reception. The phone rang and rang, but no one picked up. She dried herself and pulled some clothes on, left Jake to soak and went back down in the lift.

The reception was still deserted. There was an old-fashioned bell on the desk, the kind you had to slap with the palm of your hand, but on this occasion it summoned no one. She leaned over the desk and peered into the office behind the reception, and though all was in order, no one was there. She felt slightly queasy.

Her first instincts had been to get warm and to look after Jake, forgetting that her own ordeal had been worse than his. Although he too had been picked up by the avalanche and deposited on the slopes, he'd not been buried alive. Images from the ordeal were starting to return to her mind for the second time since Jake had dug her out of the snow. Her hands were trembling. She got back into the lift and returned to their room.

Jake had gone back to sleep in the bath. She stood in the doorway looking at him and he seemed to sense her presence. He opened his eyes.

'There's no one there.'

'Where?'

'Downstairs. I just went downstairs. There's no one there.'

'Well, the hotel is usually dead at this time, isn't it? All the guests are out.'

'What about the staff?'

'Probably off on a cigarette break.'

She looked doubtful. 'But they're not, are they?'

'Who aren't what?'

'The guests. They're not all out, are they? The slopes are closed.'

'Well, maybe the avalanche was worse than we thought it was. Maybe everyone is up on the mountain. Helping.'

'Do you think so? Do you think it was a really bad one?'

'It was bad enough for us. I mean, I've no idea. Maybe we just got caught in a tiny wing of the main avalanche. What can we do?' He stepped out of the bath and reached for a towel. 'All we can do is wait until they come back.'

She went through to the bedroom and sat on the bed, twisting her fingers.

Jake appeared wrapped in his towel, his pink skin still steaming slightly from the warmth of the bath. 'There must be a rule,' he said, 'that says a man shouldn't find his wife so dirty-sexy. Especially after a near-death experience.'

He whipped the towel off and upended her on the bed, lifting her legs in the air. She shrieked, and when he launched himself on top of her she fought back. He winced.

'My ribs.'

'Serves you right.'

22

'We nearly died! We nearly died. I want to be all over you. Like that avalanche.'

'Come here.'

'I'm getting hungry. Where's that steak, dripping with blood? To hell with the prices, let's rustle up some room service.' He studied the menu. 'What do you want ordering?'

'Rare steak, yes. Red wine. Anything that's bad for you.'

He dialled the number for room service. There was no answer, so he dialled the reception desk. No one picked up. 'Odd.'

'I told you, there's no one there. You don't listen.

He hung on to the phone a while longer. Then with a gentle click he laid the receiver back on its cradle. 'Let's get dressed. We can get something at the restaurant.'

On their way to the restaurant, Zoe got an attack of the giggles. She put her hand over her mouth but a pig-snort came out. Jake stopped in the corridor and looked at her, but the quizzical expression on his face only made her worse. Maybe it was hysteria after the close encounter with death, but something made Zoe want to laugh now. Not smile, or giggle, but laugh. The urge to laugh at nothing was uncontrollable.

There was an uninspiring abstract print on the wall near the lift and this made her want to laugh. The silly musical chime of the lift arriving on the third floor made her want to laugh, too. There was something absurd about these vapid decorations that stood in vivid contrast to where she'd just been, upended in the snow. The mirrors in the lift made her want to laugh. The notice about the weight capacity of the lift; the strip of carpet on the floor; the alarm button. It all seemed so ridiculous she wanted to guffaw.

'What?' said Jake. 'What?'

She slammed herself back against the mirror in the lift and howled, convulsing, holding her ribs.

'No, I'm glad you find it all so amusing,' said Jake. 'I do too. Sort of. We nearly died. That's hugely entertaining. You're cracked.'

Almost to shut her up he pressed her against the wall of the lift and put his tongue inside her mouth. She felt her own convulsions discharging through Jake, like a power source. She felt him hard against her. They'd only just fucked and he wanted her again. She wanted him again, too.

The lift reached the reception and the doors opened. Zoe pushed him off her, flicked her hair and composed herself before stepping out of the lift.

She needn't have bothered. There was still nobody there.

They crossed to the reception desk. Jake hit the bell. 'Shop!' he shouted, mugging at her.

'Let's try the restaurant.'

They passed the neat but vacant concierge's desk of blond wood and walked through to the hotel restaurant. The dining room was habitually quiet during the daytime, with most of the guests eating there in the evening only, but one or two tables were usually occupied.

Not today.

The lights were up everywhere, but all the tables were empty. A sign at the entrance to the dining room directed guests to wait to be seated by the maître d', but there was no maître d', and there were no waiters. The restaurant was set perfectly for business: crisp linen tablecloths and napkins, heavy crystal wine glasses, silver cutlery, all spotlessly presented. Faint muzak piped overhead.

Jake stood with his hands on his hips. He turned back and forth and then headed towards the kitchens. He stepped through the swing doors, and Zoe followed.

There was no kitchen staff. The clean stainless-steel work surfaces were primed with freshly chopped vegetables and cuts of red meat, all as if ready to be prepared for lunch. On the far side of the kitchen an industrial-sized stainless-steel dishwasher had been loaded with dirty breakfast plates and dishes. Jake opened the door of a giant freezer cabinet and was hit by a blast of cold air. After a quick glance inside he closed the door.

Zoe touched him on the forearm. 'Do you think we should leave?'

'Leave?'

'Leave the hotel.'

'Why would we do that?'

'Here's what I think. This hotel lies at the foot of the avalanche slope. It lies right in the path of the snow. After this morning's avalanche they've evacuated everyone. Look around you: it's been cleared in five minutes flat. I think we're in danger here. I think we'd better go.'

Jake blinked. 'Christ. Okay, let's get our coats. We'll walk into the village.'

'And let's just pray it doesn't come down on our heads right now.'

'You pray if you like. I'd rather just fret.'

'Oh shut up.'

*

So they left the hotel and walked into the village of Saint-Bernard. Normally there was a shuttle service: a minibus running regularly on the half-hour covered the distance in six or seven minutes. Walking took about thirty.

The road was silent. It was still snowing. The light had changed and the snow on the ground had an eerie blue-grey tint. Any footprints or tracks had been almost covered by fresh, soft, feathery snow.

On the previous evening they had made their way from the hotel into town on foot. It had been a memorable walk. The snowy path was lined with spruce and fir trees exhaling a sappy perfume, and the way was illuminated, at one-hundred-metre intervals, by the soft orange glow of graceful wrought-iron lamp posts. They'd been passed en route by an enormous black horse pulling a sledge carrying a couple of happy but bashful tourists. Steam rose from the great horse's flanks and plumes of vapour billowed from its nostrils as it trotted through the thick snow. The couple in the sledge had waved shyly.

But today the route seemed dangerous. They walked briskly, not talking, both straining their ears for the sounds of the mountain. Because there were warning sounds. A distant *crump*, way up high, like a single round of gunfire. A creaking. A kind of groan, like a great weight shifting on the mountain itself. A breeze that became a sigh through the snow itself. All could be premonitions of sliding snow.

They said nothing to each other, but Zoe took Jake's hand, and they quickened their pace. The crunch and squeak of their snow boots was no comfort. Even those small sounds seemed like an affront to the mountain, the squeak of a mouse to an elephant. A challenge.

'Can you feel the pressure?' Zoe said. 'In the air? It's like I can feel the weight of the snow on the mountain.'

'You're imagining it. Just keep walking.'

'I'm not imagining it. The air is thick. Like something is going to happen.'

'Nothing is going to happen.'

'So why have they evacuated the hotel, arsehole?'

'Precaution. It would be bloody bad luck, wouldn't it, to survive one avalanche and then get caught in another?'

'Yeah. Bloody bad luck happens.'

'Not today it won't.'

'You're going to protect me, Jake?'

'With my bare hands.'

Then from above them came the unmistakable groan, the sound of snow sliding, like a folding of great sheets of metal.

Zoe stopped in her tracks. 'Oh God!'

'It's okay. Come on, keep moving. It's just the snow shifting.'

'Oh really? That's what I'm afraid of – the snow damn well shifting! Snow shifting is called an avalanche, isn't it?'

'Shh! Talk quietly. What I mean is that the snow does it all the time. That's why they have snowploughs on the pistes. Because the snow shifts and banks. It doesn't mean it's coming down right now.'

'Yeah? You know about these things? You're a veterinary surgeon. How come you're an expert in shifting snow? You're just bullshitting.'

'That's right, I'm bullshitting.'

'Why? Why are you bullshitting?'

He stopped and turned to her. 'It's what I do when I get frightened, okay? I bullshit. It's an effective way of making things seem better. There, are you happy now you've seen through me? Can we carry on walking now that my failure as a human being has been exposed? Well?'

The snow on the mountain slope groaned again overhead. There was a further inexplicable sound like great fishing nets cast into the sea. She slipped her arm inside his and they hiked on into the village under the soft orange glow of the lamps.

There was no one on the streets. A number of cars were parked near the centre of the village, but they were all topped with a flat cake-like layer of snow from the day's precipitation. The village was spooky-quiet. They came upon another small hotel, called the Petit la Creu. Snow had drifted against the foot of the entrance door.

They pushed their way in, the heavy draught excluders on the bottom of the door dragging against the floor. The reception was warm, almost stifling. Lights were blazing everywhere but the reception was deserted. Exactly like their own hotel.

'Do you think the whole village has been evacuated?' asked Zoe.

'Have you got that girl's number?'

'What girl?'

'That dozy girl.'

'What dozy girl?'

'The rep. The company rep. The one who was on the bus from the airport. The one who couldn't stop smiling. Didn't she flip you a card with her number?'

Zoe unzipped her handbag and took out her purse. She sorted through her plastic credit cards and club cards to find the rep's business card. 'I don't have it. You must have it.'

'I don't have it. She gave it you.'

'She didn't give it me. I haven't got it. I remember at the time she had a twinkle in her eye when she handed it to you. So you must have it.'

'What twinkle?'

'*You* had it!'

'All right! Keep your hair on!' Jake unbuttoned his jacket, unzipped his inner breast pocket and took out his wallet. There among his credit cards he found the holiday company business card with the rep's mobile phone number.

'I told you you had it. You fancy her.'

'Yep, I like a woman who smiles. They're rare in these parts.'

'Give it me.'

ELFINDA CARTER, SENIOR TOUR REPRESENTATIVE

WINTERTOURS HOLIDAYS

TEL: 07797 551737

'Anyway, what kind of a name is Elfinda?' she said.

'Maybe she's an elf.'

'Elfinda the twinkling elf, apparently.'

'You embarrassed us.'

When Elfinda the rep had offered her card she had asked for Jake's number in return. It was routine, should the company need to contact them about trips and events. Zoe, tired of all the twinkling in the air, had leaned across and shoved, instead, her own card into the startled rep's hands.

'Embarrassed us? I should have kicked her skinny arse.'

Zoe reached across the reception desk and picked up the telephone. There was a strong dialling tone. She tapped out the numbers printed on the card. The phone rang and she crossed her legs as she waited for someone to pick up.

The phone rang for a long time before it finally rang off.

'No one there?'

'No one there. Elf or otherwise.'

'There's a police station in the village, behind the supermarket. We should go there anyway. See what's happening.'

They left the Petit la Creu and trudged through the village, past the pretty church with its slender tower, taking a right-hand turn down a side street towards the supermarket and the police station. They passed no one. Neither was there any activity in any of the shops. Some of the stores were illuminated, some were not. The lights were all on in the supermarket, but there were no people, neither customers nor staff, to be seen through the windows.

A four-wheel-drive police vehicle with snow chains on its tyres was parked in the yard. The police station itself was a small, unprepossessing concrete building almost hiding behind the supermarket. They pushed open the heavy glass and steel door, and then opened a second door onto a small space furnished with a white melamine reception desk and three moulded plastic chairs.

Jake shouted loudly. This time he didn't call *Shop!*

Zoe stepped behind the melamine counter, to a door behind it plastered with posters and notices. She tapped on the door, and when no one answered she pushed it open. There was a cramped office equipped with a couple of desks, PCs, a printer, a bank of filing cabinets, a coffee machine. The red light on the coffee machine was switched on, and half a pot of coffee was still warming. There was an anteroom visible with a coat rack and a police coat hanging on a peg.

'Hello!'

They sat at the police desks for half an hour, hands dug into their coat pockets, trying to figure out what to do.

'Okay,' Jake said. 'The entire village has been evacuated. Why? Avalanche risk. That's the explanation. Sometimes these avalanches – big avalanches, not the kind we got caught in this morning – can take out an entire village like this. Happened near Chamonix a few years ago and pushed over twenty chalets. And all this snow falling has increased the risk. So everyone's gone.'

'How come they just left us?'

'Maybe they thought we were killed in the avalanche this morning.'

'Wouldn't there be rescue teams?'

'Look, I don't know. All I know is the place has been evacuated, and we need to get out of here and pretty quick.'

'Right. How?' Zoe said.

'That's the ... that's just it. We can walk. We could get some skis from a store and try to make it further down the mountain. But I don't much fancy that, given what we know, and given what happened this morning.'

'Me neither.'

'Or we can drive. Which means we just take one of these cars parked in the village. Drive slow, so it doesn't trigger anything.'

'Right. We'll do that.'

'Right.'

'Let's go then.'

'So what are we waiting for, Zoe?'

'I don't know. I'm scared.'

'Scared? There's nowt to be scared about, you big girl's blouse. Nowt at all. Actually I'm scared, too. Never mind all that. Look, we've got to find a car with keys still in the ignition.'

'Right. Couldn't we—'

'Couldn't we what? Hot-wire a car like they do in the movies?'

'Yes.'

'You know how to do it?'

'You're the technical one. You're the man.'

'Well, I'll tell you something for nothing, fuckwit of a wife. I don't know how to hot-wire a car. As you correctly pointed out I'm a vet, I work with dogs and white mice and budgerigars and in all my training and experience as a vet, for some reason I've never been called upon to hot-wire a car. To save our bacon. Until now.'

'Don't get exercised with me.'

'I'll tell you another thing for nothing. See how they do it in the movies? They just rip out some wires from under the dashboard and stick 'em together and the car coughs into life? A car mechanic told me that's all bollocks. It doesn't work like that any more. He said if you do that the most likely thing that'll happen is you'll give yourself an electric shock.'

'So we won't do that.'

'And he was a car mechanic. A proper car mechanic.'

'So, as you said, we go and look for a car that still has the keys in it. And then we drive out. With the engine sort of muffled.'

'You're a sarcastic bitch, you know that?'

'It's why you married me. You love it.'

But before leaving the police station they tried, once more, the telephone number of Elfinda the smiling holiday rep. Just as with their earlier attempt, the phone rang off before anyone answered.

Outside, and with the snow falling more heavily around them now, they went from car to car, trying the drivers' doors, looking for one that would open. They tried perhaps fifty or sixty vehicles and did find doors open on four of them; but none had the keys inside.

The snow came down heavier still, and with it an oyster-coloured mist. They were starting to feel both cold and tired.

'I've just thought of something,' Jake said.

'What?'

'Back at the police station – there was a police car. Maybe the keys are in the office.'

'What, steal a police car? Don't even think about it.'

'But the situation is somewhat exceptional, surely?'

Zoe knitted her eyebrows but followed him back down the hill to the police station. There they found the keys to the police car, hanging on a hook by the door.

'Are you sure it's okay to just ... take it?'

'No.'

The police car fired into life first time, kicking out a lot of diesel smoke. They had to scrape snow from the windshield and de-ice the glass. Jake steered the car out of the police yard and onto the street. He honked the horn a few times; he was expecting a hand on his collar at any moment, and if the police did return to see their car being stolen he wanted to be able to say that he had hardly been stealthy about the operation.

He drove slowly past the supermarket, unused to the weight of the 4WD vehicle. In order to leave the village the way they had come in from the airport, they would have to drive past their hotel. Zoe wanted to stop and gather their things; Jake didn't because the snow was coming down even heavier now, and the blanket of mist was getting thicker by the moment. Visibility was already less than twenty metres.

'We need our passports, hon, and there are things I don't want to leave. Come on, Jake. Two minutes.'

'If we end up dead because of these two minutes, I'll kill you.'

'Fair enough.'

They pulled up outside the deserted hotel. Jake left the engine running, exhaust smoke billowing in the freezing air, as they got out. They rode the lift up to the third floor in silence, where their arrival was heralded by a tiny ping. Once in the room they opened their suitcases on the bed, flung everything in without care and clicked them shut. Then they took the suitcases down and out to the car, stowing them on the rear seat.

Jake growled. The mist had thickened. It was still oyster-grey and he fancied that it had an iridescent sheen where the electric light was caught and refracted: at another time, beautiful. The snow hadn't abated either. It fell like thick, soft goose-feathers: the kind of snow that would have delighted any skier, but right now it was the last thing they wanted.

Visibility had dropped to about ten metres. He could only vaguely discern the shape of the buildings across the road from the hotel. What's more, it was already late afternoon. Even without the snow the daylight was beginning to fade. Prospects for driving were not good. He would need to get a move on if they were to reach anywhere useful before the daylight winked out; and yet Jake felt the crushing potential of triggering the big avalanche if he drove faster than a crawl.

They set off at a cautious pace. Giant flakes of snow landed on the windscreen as the car made it's laborious way along the mountain road. Then he bumped something in the road.

'What was that?'

'Don't know. I think I hit the kerbstone.'

'Keep away from the kerbstone. Drive in the middle of the road.'

'Gosh, I hadn't thought of that! Thanks for that well-considered advice. Driving in the middle of the road is exactly what I'm trying to do.'

But pretty soon he bumped a kerbstone again. It was impossible. He complained that he couldn't see a thing now in the fading light. They talked about turning around but decided they had to press on. Half a kilometre or so further along the road, the car bumped, jolted and shuddered. They had driven clean off the road.

Jake jammed on the brakes. The car skidded and juddered to a halt. Leaving the engine still running, he got out of the car, but with the ground invisible under his feet he dropped a few centimetres and turned his ankle.

'Careful as you get out!' he shouted to Zoe.

She stepped out of the car and came round to join him. The front wheel on the driver's side was hanging in free space. The other three wheels were fixed on rocky, snowy terrain. Jake looked down. He had no way of knowing if the drop under the driver's-side wheel was one metre or a hundred. The misty whiteness of not knowing flashed through him like a blade.

'Can we reverse out?' Zoe asked.

'Maybe we could, but I don't want to drive any further in this fog.'

'What? We have to go, Jake!'

He pointed to the car's dangling wheel. 'Got any idea what's under there? I don't. We can't drive. I remember when we came here on the bus: most of the mountain road drops clean away on one side. There's no barrier to keep you on the road, Zoe! It's straight over the edge.'

'Then we have to walk.'

'Okay. We can walk.'

Zoe knew Jake well enough to hear an unspoken *but* in his sentences. 'But ...' she filled in for him.

'But here's what I think. We'll be walking into the night and into sub-zero temperatures. We could probably stay on the road, if we're careful. But it's twenty kilometres to the next village. We haven't eaten anything all day and I'm already fucking freezing. In addition to the risk of dying of exposure on the mountain, we have the serious threat of an avalanche sweeping us off the road. Now, I know the hotel isn't safe. But it's a massive concrete building, and being inside there has got be safer than being out here.'

'Jesus!'

'You know I'm right.'

'Are we going to drive back?'

He looked at the overhanging wheel. 'No. I reckon we check this out in the morning, when the snow has stopped and we can see what we're looking at. We didn't get far. We could be back at the hotel in twenty minutes. Half an hour tops. '

She didn't argue. He switched off the engine got out and opened the back of the car. They stuffed a few essentials into a small bag and abandoned the rest before walking back in the direction of the hotel.

'Some holiday this is turning out to be,' Jake said.

'Some holiday.'

'I can just about see my hand in front of my face. No, that's not true. I can see your face. It's glowing.'

'Believe it or not I'm sweating.'

And she could see his face, too, gleaming dimly in the falling snow and the grey, darkening mist; as if his skin were illuminated from behind. His skin was like parchment in this light, she decided, holy parchment, and his glittering blue eyes and his nut-brown eyebrows and the hint of crimson of his lips were like a monk's illustrations on a sacred manuscript.

'What you looking at?'

'You. I love you.'

He laughed. 'How can you think of that at a time like this? I married a loon who drags me into avalanches.'

'This situation is loony, and all I can see is your lovely face, and I'm glad I can see it. I'm really, really glad.'

'Come on. Hold my hand. Let's get back to that hotel.'

3

There was a display board on the wall near the hotel reception, offering day trips, toboggan events, sleigh rides and fondue evenings. There were also contact numbers for all the holiday companies represented at the resort. Thumbtacked to the board was also a list of doctors, vets, pharmacies and all the emergency services associated with Saint-Bernard. Jake snatched the list from the board. They went back up to their room with the list and Jake began calling.

There was a good, clear, throaty dialling tone on the line. He called each of the holiday companies in turn, and in each case no one picked up. He dialled the local police station, from where they'd taken the car. No joy. He dialled the national emergency number. In none of these cases did anyone pick up the phone.

'Phone someone in England,' Zoe said. 'Phone your mother.'

Zoe's parents were both dead. Her mother had died long before Jake and Zoe had even met, though he had known her dad, Archie, for a couple of years before he too had died. Jake's elderly father, meanwhile, had died some time after divorcing his mother, the only remaining parent. She was an over-fussy but kind woman with a bad blue rinse who had moved up to Scotland shortly after an unpleasant divorce conducted while Jake was at boarding school. His mother – emotionally as well as geographically remote – had thankfully thought very highly of Zoe because she was 'musical'. Jake figured that his mother might at least contact someone in a position of authority and let them know that the pair had been left behind after the evacuation.

'She'll freak out,' Jake said, dialling the number. 'You know what she's like.'

'Phone her anyway.'

After he got no reply, Jake put the phone down. 'It's her Whist night. She always goes to Whist at the church on a Friday.'

'Lovely. I hope she gets nine tricks or whatever while we're here about to be eaten alive on the side of the mountain.'

'I'm going to call Simon.'

Simon was Jake's old friend from college. He was a housing officer for the local authority, and he'd been best man at their wedding; and even when Simon had tried to seduce Zoe one time somehow that relationship had survived. Jake called Simon on his mobile phone, but the signal faltered. So he called him on his landline, but that too rang off.

'What time is it? He's probably gone straight down the Jolly Miller after work. Who else can we call?'

It was a short list. They were on good terms with their neighbours at home but they were elderly and very frail. They decided against calling them. Zoe tried calling two close friends but no one picked up.

'No one is answering anywhere. They can't all be throwing back pints at the Jolly Miller! Let's switch the TV on, see if we can get some local news.'

Zoe opened the mahogany TV cabinet doors and

switched on the set. She flashed through the channels but all she could get was an electrical snowstorm of a picture and the sound of static interference. Jake got up and grabbed the remote control from her, as if his pressing the buttons might produce better results. It didn't. The TV was also programmed for radio reception, but nothing was coming through on any of the channels. Just static. White noise.

'Look,' Zoe said, 'I'm not thinking straight. We're here for the night. We need to eat something.'

'We'll have to cook it ourselves.'

'No hardship. Let's see what they've got in the kitchen.'

They went down to the restaurant and slipped through to the kitchens, where they'd been earlier. Everything was still the way they'd found it on their first visit. Lean cuts of red meat lay on the work counter, ready for cooking, as did a neat array of chopped vegetables. They decided to leave the stuff that had been out all day. In the chiller cabinet they found fresh fillet steaks.

Zoe poured olive oil into a huge pan while Jake popped the gas burners. He found a pristine white chef's toque and put it on. He was living it large. 'Everything's runnin'. Gas. Light. Me. We may be about to die under an avalanche but I'm in the kitchen and we're sizzling a steak.'

He served it medium rare with onions and mushrooms. Zoe meanwhile dished up green beans and butter. She had also raided the wine store and popped open a bottle of red.

'What's this, you cheapskate? Get back and fetch us a bottle of real wine, will ya?'

Zoe shook her head. 'Take that hat off. You look

like a twat. We'll get billed for all this, you know.'

'I don't care. If this is my last bottle of wine I want something good.'

He got up. When he came back she'd lit a candle at the table. He was still wearing his toque, and was carrying a bottle of Châteauneuf-du-Pape. She wanted to look at the wine list to see what his choice might have cost them, but he grabbed it off her and skimmed it across the empty restaurant, telling her to just pour it. She in turn snatched the toque from his head and tossed it the way of the wine list.

'We'll get thrown out of here,' he said, clinking glasses.

'Survivors,' she said.

'Survivors.'

'This is surreal.'

'But it's not a dream.'

'When I think of all the places we've had dinner together. Meals at home. Dinners out. Fancy restaurants. Cheap cafés. Picnics. This is the one I'll remember above any of them. It's like we're the last people in the world.'

'And the snow outside is still falling. If you were with the right person you might even find this romantic.'

The candlelight wavered slightly, and she saw the catch-light flicker in his bloodshot eyes, and she remembered that they had come on this holiday with a job to do. There was something they had to sort out. Something they were meant to discuss. But she knew that right now was the wrong moment. She let it go.

'How's your steak?'

'Perfect. You know,' he said, 'I think I've always been secretly afraid of the avalanche. This is what, almost my twentieth skiing break? And right from when

I was a beginner I've always known it was there. Like something in your dreams, crouched, waiting behind you, waiting to snatch it all away from you.'

'Are you still afraid of it? After what happened today?'

'Put it like this. I think we should move into one of the rooms across the hall. I really don't think the snow is going to crash down on us. But if it did, we'd be safer on that side.'

'Right. That's a very nice wine.'

'Really? Doesn't taste of much to me.'

'Nonsense. Let's go two bottles.'

'You sure? I don't want you drunk.'

'Yes you do. You want me drunk.'

They commandeered a new room, where they lay on the bed with the curtains open, should there be any movement or activity or patrols in the night. Zoe was anxious at every creak of the hotel, in case it heralded the big slide of snow. Jake was oddly resigned. He didn't think it was going to happen: he didn't know why he thought that, he just felt that despite the evacuation, it wasn't a threat.

Two bottles of red wine were enough to sedate them, though sleep didn't come easily. They lay kissing for hours. Just kissing, not wanting to speak, not wanting to take their mouths away from each other's lips, which was of course a way of speaking. Then Jake did something he'd never done before, which was to lift her and carry her from the bed so that they fucked against the wall, standing up, with Zoe balanced on her toes.

Then they fell back into bed, and finally fell asleep.

*

42

'Wake up!'

Jake blinked at her. It was morning. Zoe pulled off her wool hat and opened her ski jacket. She'd been outside, to a pharmacy, to get some drops for their bloodshot eyes.

'You been out?'

'I got you this. Put your head back and open your eyes. Man, that looks sore. Your eyes are like piss-holes in the snow.' She let three drops fall into each of his eyes, then screwed the dropper back into the bottle.

'Anyone out there?'

'Nope.'

'What time is it?'

'Not late.'

Jake tossed back the covers. 'You shouldn't have let me sleep.'

'I thought you needed it. I think you're still traumatised.'

'I'm not.'

'I think you are. You're behaving differently.'

'Like how?'

Zoe raised an eyebrow.

He dressed hurriedly. 'We need to get that car back on the road and get going.'

'Okay. I brought you some breakfast from the kitchen.'

There was a tray on the table: coffee, juice and scrambled eggs on toast under a silver dome. 'You know what? You could almost get to like it here. If you didn't have to scarper.'

He ate breakfast quickly, pulled on his thermal underwear, his salopettes and ski jacket and together they went out to take a look at the car. It was still snowing but only very lightly now. Tiny flakes billowed in the air, barely contributing to the thick, feathery deposit that layered the road and the pavement. There were plenty of patches of blue in the sky between the low-lying grey clouds. They stuck to the middle of the road, trudging through the thick snow.

After twenty minutes they came upon the police car and Zoe gasped as if she'd been punched in the stomach.

'Holy heaven!'

Jake just blinked.

The wheel of the police car on the driver's side dangled in space above a clean drop of fifteen metres down a smooth face of granite. Had it continued over, the car would have hit more granite rocks at the bottom, and from there it would have plunged down a steep tree-lined slope. Maybe it would have hit a tree trunk head on; maybe not. A rounded tooth of amber-stained limestone poking out of the snow in front of the passenger-side wheel had stopped any further onward motion of the car. The rock blocking the wheel looked like a carved tombstone, but their names weren't chiselled there because it had been their salvation.

Zoe kneeled on the snow and covered her ears with her hands. 'I don't believe it.'

'You'd better.'

'We must have an angel watching over us. I swear.'

'Well, I don't believe in angels. But you're right.'

Zoe scrambled to her feet again and grabbed Jake's arm. They stared down at the car, and the drop beneath it, without another word.

Jake was trying to calculate if he might be able to reverse the police car back onto the road. The front passenger wheel was blocked, sure enough, but the vehicle was pointing downwards and looked ready to slip sideways. The prospect of climbing into the car, starting the engine and trying to back out was terrifying.

He watched Zoe go round to the driver's side. 'No,' he said.

'Maybe it will.'

'Don't even think about it.'

They walked back to the village discussing alternatives. They could try to find another vehicle. It was entirely possible that there might be more keys hanging around in one of the many stores that remained unlocked. Or they could simply walk out and follow the road across the mountain.

There were cars parked near their hotel. They checked them all out. They were all locked. They knew their chances of finding an unlocked car with its keys dangling in the ignition were pretty slim, but not impossible.

Yet within just twenty minutes they found a car with its keys winking in the ignition. Jake swung into the driver's seat and turned the key, but the battery was completely flat. They tried bump-starting the car on a short hill, but nothing happened. They abandoned the car at the bottom of the rise and resumed their search.

Jake let out a cry when he stumbled upon a parking lot with eighteen identical black snowmobiles. 'Here's our ride out!' he shouted. 'Take your pick, they all look the same.'

But his enthusiasm was premature. All eighteen snowmobiles were linked by a thick chain and a massive padlock. They could find neither keys for the snowmobiles nor the key for the padlock. The search briefly turned to thoughts of a bolt-cropper, but this idea was abandoned when they realised that even if they did find a bolt-cropper they still had no ignition keys.

After three hours they were ready to admit defeat, at least for the day.

'What will we do?' Zoe asked.

'Do? We'll go back to our room in the hotel for another night. Drink some more of their fuckin' fabulous tasteless wine. Then we'll get up bright and early and we'll hike out of here once and for all by following the road.'

They linked arms, and in a kind of neurasthenic trance they trudged back to the hotel.

They used the sauna to get warm again, and then swam in the spa pool. The water made a hollow lapping noise in the absence of any other guests; the changing rooms echoed oddly; the padding of their feet on the tiles was a lonely sound.

Afterwards they spent an hour using the hotel's computers to get online. The computers failed to connect. While Zoe persisted in her efforts, Jake went through the entire series of phone numbers all over again. One by one the lines rang and rang and no one answered. No one answered anywhere.

'It's the local exchange. The fault has to lie with the local exchange,' Jake said. 'It must be out of commission otherwise somebody would pick up.'

They were no more successful with their mobile phones.

Jake found the toque Zoe had thrown on the floor

and cooked again that night. He defrosted chicken and discovered spices to rustle up a sweet-and-sour stir-fry. He found a CD player and cranked the volume up high, banging pots and pans and cracking the imaginary heads of poor little kitchen boys to get his spirits up. There was a CD of classical operatic stuff sitting in the machine, offering a soaring mezzo-soprano diva vocalising beautiful words he couldn't understand. He turned up the burners on the cooker and flamed oil in a skillet as if it was all theatre.

The stainless-steel kitchen work surface still offered the lean cuts of meat and chopped vegetables laid out from yesterday. Everything looked and smelled as fresh as if it had just been prepared moments earlier, but he left it lying there and cleaned himself another work surface across the kitchen.

Zoe sat at the table in the restaurant; the table was laid, with crisp linen and silver cutlery all in place. Her hands were folded under her chin. She'd found a bottle of champagne.

'Don't ask the price. We'll hide the empty bottle. No one will ever know.'

With the operatic vocals soaring above their candle-lit table and the darkness thickening outside, they ate their second meal in the deserted restaurant. The music had a phantom beauty, swooping between the empty rows of tables. Without a word Zoe got up and changed it, pointedly, for some upbeat Pixies tunes.

'Why has no one come for us?' she said.

'I don't know. I don't know.'

The champagne went to Zoe's head. They guzzled it, and Zoe fetched a second bottle.

'Enjoy this,' she said, pouring freely, 'because the

47

cost of those two bottles amounts to roughly the same as the cost of this holiday.'

'You're joking.'

'I'm not. They're on what's called the "reserve list".'

'What's a "reserve list"?'

'Well, there's the wine list and then there's the reserve list. It's for special occasions. If you can't find anything expensive enough on the wine list you ask for the reserve list. It's for special people with a discerning palate and a big fat arse.'

'You do realise we're going to get landed for this?'

'No we're not. We'll deny everything. And I'll tell you something else. For these two nights I've felt like you and I were the last two people on earth. I have you totally to myself, with not even a waitress to distract you. And some perverse part of me has really enjoyed it. Tomorrow it's going to be over and there will be things I'll wish I'd said to you when I had you to myself.'

'Like what?'

'Like how long ago was the avalanche?'

'Uh? Only yesterday morning. Incredibly.'

'Exactly. Only yesterday morning. And it feels like an incredibly long time ago.'

'You're right. It does.'

'A long time ago since we almost lost each other. We almost died, Jake. And every second since then seems to have expanded, and it's because there's just you ...' She held her glass up, a little unsteadily, to clink it with his. 'And me.' She looked around the empty restaurant. 'Everyone else sucks our time from us. I could almost stay here a few more days, just out of bloody-mindedness.'

'Do you think we're on a reserve list?'

'What?'

'God's reserve list. Nature's reserve list. Like everyone else is on the ordinary menu and we've been kept back here cos we're on the reserve list.'

'That's a weird idea.'

He half-smiled at her. 'All the other people will be back soon.'

'I know. And we'll leave first thing in the morning. Come on, let's go to bed.'

'You're drunk.'

'Bring the rest of that bottle since it cost so bloody much.'

She was indeed drunk. When the elevator doors opened she pushed him inside and lunged at him. With the lift doors closing she leapt on him and bit his lip, fumbling with his belt and hoiking down his trousers. Falling to her knees she fellated him. His elbow hit the lift buttons and the doors opened.

Jake froze. 'Excuse me, sir,' he said, 'my wife will be finished in a moment.'

Zoe stopped and looked up as if she half-expected to see a shocked guest in the lobby. She took a swig of bubbling champagne from the bottle, swallowed, and put his dick back in her mouth.

The elevator bell chimed and the doors closed again.

'Wake up.'

Zoe groaned. Her head felt like someone had split it with an ice-axe. Jake was dressed, standing over her, holding a mug of gently steaming coffee under her nose.

'What time is it?'

'Time to go.'

'Really?'

'It's snowing again. We don't want to leave it too late. We're going to have to hike for maybe four hours before we get to the next village. It's snowing heavily and with all this snow coming down, all the time we're here the avalanche risk increases. So please get your sweet, shiny arse out of that bed.'

'That cheap champagne went to my head,' she said, dragging herself off to the shower.

He'd brought up a breakfast of toast and rolls, and cheese and salami. He'd packed a rucksack. While she slept he'd been out and found the rucksack, a torch and a magnetic compass in a store.

Before they left she made him sit and tilt back his head while she applied eye-drops. 'You still look like a zombie. Red then blue then black. Like an archery target.'

'That's not an archery target.'

'Oh shut up. Now you do me.'

They were out on the road by seven-thirty that morning. The snow had thickened. The clouds overhead were like buckled steel and though the flakes were light they were falling in thick profusion. A fine mist came along with it.

They followed the road. Pretty soon they passed the police car with its wheel dangling over the precipice. The snow had made a thick crust on the windscreen and on the bonnet. Jake stopped and looked at the vehicle wistfully. The mist was thickening and Zoe told him not to even think about it.

The road climbed steeply. After another half an hour of ascending the mountain road the snow-mist became impenetrable. It had that same oyster-grey quality, with traces of iridescence where the light played. They walked on steadily, but couldn't see where they were going.

Jake stepped off the road and turned his ankle.

'I don't like it,' Zoe said. 'We're walking blind.'

'It's okay. I'm okay. We just follow the tarmac.'

'I can't even see the tarmac. Or feel it underneath me.'

Jake took his compass out of his bag. He squatted down and placed it on his knee. 'That's north and we want to go west. This is okay. Let's press on.'

There was confidence in his voice, but Zoe neither shared it nor trusted it. He was made of different stuff from her. He'd had an upbringing that had taught him to simulate confidence when he didn't feel it in his bones, and she knew the difference. She had been taught to trust her instincts, and to be guided by them. She thought that her way got it right or wrong just as much as his way.

They took it slowly, holding hands, sometimes following the outer curve of the road. The road twisted wildly, a serpentine track winding around and across the mountain, and they followed it almost blind, reduced to a shuffling pace. Then Zoe must have put a foot off the road because her boot went through snow up to her thigh.

'This scares me, Jake. It scares me. I feel like we could easily walk off the road. Why don't we take shelter for half an hour? See if the mist lifts a little?'

'It's not going to lift.'

'How the hell do you know that?'

'This is in for the day. You can see that. If we hunker down we'll just get cold. We have to press on.'

So they did. And after another ten minutes there came a gust of wind that for a tantalising moment revealed the road parting in opposite directions. Then the image of the parting in the road was instantly swallowed up by the thick mist. The snow came down harder.

Jake squatted in the road again and took out his compass.

'What's this?'

Zoe squatted beside him, peering at the compass. The needle was circling the compass, hunting.

'You haven't got it level. Put it down flat.'

Jake cleared some snow from the road with his ski gauntlet and placed the compass down on the snow. The needle continued to hunt, moving steadily clockwise across the face of the compass. Then it stopped. Almost immediately it resumed its hunting, now moving anticlockwise.

'What does that mean?' Zoe said.

Jake didn't answer.

She grabbed it; shook it; put it down on the snow again. The needle continued to hunt for its magnetic home, without coming to rest.

'It's fucked.'

'It was working fine when I picked it up,' Jake said. 'It was working fine.'

'Right.'

'It was. It was working fine.'

'Nevertheless.'

'Nevertheless? What does that mean? Nevertheless?'

'It means we're turning back.'

'Like hell!'

'Jake, we've been walking for what, an hour? We haven't gone more than a kilometre or two. If you think we're going to get anywhere in this you're stupid. I'm not carrying on in this. And as you say, we can't stay here.'

She turned from him and began to retrace her steps. Within seconds they couldn't see each other. After a moment he started yelling after her.

'I'm just here!' she shouted.

He loomed out of the mist and grabbed her coat. 'Don't do that, Zoe!'

'Don't do what?'

'Don't just walk off like that! We have to stay together. You don't seem to realise that I could lose you in this. It could happen in seconds! This is the mountain and there's no one around! No one! This isn't a walk to the shops!'

'Okay.'

'You have to respect the mountain.'

'I said okay, didn't I?'

They stood in the billowing snow, their noses perhaps fifteen centimetres apart but barely making out the expression on the other's face. In the mist, each appeared to the other like a faded and fading grey photograph.

'We're going back,' said Zoe.

4

'Damn thing is working fine now.' Back in their hotel room, Jake sat at the table, playing with the magnetic compass. Each time he moved it, the needle wobbled and returned to train its pointer towards magnetic north.

Zoe gazed out of the window, in a kind of trance. 'It's clearing. A little.'

'I can't explain that. Why is it working fine now?'

Zoe wanted him to stop talking about the compass. Her point was that to follow the dial of even an accurate compass, you had to be able to see where you were going.

'It's like there's a conspiracy,' Jake said, 'to keep us here. Look at that: bastard thing's working perfectly.'

Zoe leapt up. 'Look at this shithole of a room! Where's the maid when you need one? Come on – help me clean up a bit.'

'Why? We're not staying.'

'We might have to, for another night at least.'

He checked the window. 'You said yourself it's clearing. And even if we have to stay we could just use another room.'

'You do what you want. I'm cleaning up.'

Zoe began to stack their used dishes on the trays they'd bought up from the kitchen. She scraped plates into the bin and pointedly set the empty plates and dishes on a tray in the middle of the table, where Jake's compass clearly indicated the way to its magnetic home. Jake put the instrument away.

She began to strip the duvet and sheets from the bed. 'Help me remake this bed.'

'I don't know why we're remaking a bed when—'

He didn't get to finish his sentence because there was a slight flutter in the air, and then a tremor started to shake the hotel. The doors of the wardrobe and the TV cabinet began to shiver on their brass hinges. Zoe froze and looked at Jake.

There followed a vast, hollow, doom-laden groan from somewhere high above them, high on the mountain slope. The hotel's foundations trembled and there came a booming and the vibration of an impact that felt as if someone were banging not on the hotel wall but on the sky, or on the wall of life itself.

'Come here!' Jake shouted. 'Come here!'

Zoe scrambled across the bed. He threw his arms around her and flung her to the floor, rolling her as close to the bed as possible. The booming shook the hotel and then stopped abruptly.

They were breathing heavily in each other's arms.

'Is it gone?' she whispered.

'I think.'

'Can we get up?'

'Maybe.'

'What was it?' she asked, not making any effort to rise from the floor.

'Avalanche. A big mother. Let's get up.'

They scrambled to their feet, then shared another long hug.

'Well, now we know why they evacuated the place,' Jake said.

'We already knew that, didn't we?'

'Yeah, we already knew that. We just doubled our knowledge.'

'I think it's cleared enough to try again,' Zoe said.

Jake looked out of the window. 'I don't know about that.'

'We're not waiting around for that snow to sweep the village away. We're not doing that. Look, wait here.'

'Where you going?'

'I'll be a few minutes. Relax.'

'I'm already relaxed,' Jake said. 'If I was any more relaxed I'd be sleeping. Christ, I'm so fucking relaxed.' He picked up the compass again.

Zoe let herself out of the hotel room and got into the elevator. In her pocket she fingered the keys to the police car. She knew she had to go and recover the car alone and without telling him; Jake would never let her risk it.

In truth the mist had cleared, and the snow was falling more lightly again. Visibility was restored – or at least reasonable – for driving, and anyway it was unlikely that they would encounter other traffic on the way into the next town. There was just the small problem of recovering the police vehicle from the road-side.

She quickened her pace. She knew exactly where the police car had gone over the edge because she'd passed it twice that very morning: once on the way in their aborted attempt to get out of the village, and once on the way back. In less than twenty minutes she could make out the snow-covered shape of the vehicle higher up the mountain road.

But there was something else up there with the car, something she couldn't at first make out. Two cylindrical black shapes protruded from the roof of the car, jet-black against the white of the snow. Zoe stopped for a moment, squinting at the unrecognisable shapes. Unable to make them out, she quickened her pace towards the car.

As she drew nearer, one of the two shapes moved fractionally; or at least appeared to move. No more than a slight adjustment to the right. Zoe slowed as she approached, then realised to her astonishment that she was looking at two very large sleek black crows that had settled on the car's roof.

Perhaps she ought to have been pleased to see the birds. They were the first other living things she'd set eyes on since they'd been caught in the avalanche. But the creatures looked both uninterested and vaguely threatening at the same time. Zoe knew she ought to be able to walk towards the dark birds and that they would immediately fly off. But they looked unusually large.

She felt a sensation of revulsion and with it a flutter of fear.

She clapped her hands together, to frighten the crows away. Her ski gauntlets merely deadened the sound, so she took them off and tried again, clapping her hands loudly as she took a hesitant step towards the car. There was a slight stirring in the dark feathers of one of the hooded black birds, and the creature seemed to peck at something moving under its feathers. The birds showed no sign of being intimidated.

Zoe was no more than four or five metres from the car, but she'd come to a halt. The truth was the birds terrified her. The crows regarded her steadily from their perch on the roof of the police car. One of them held its yellow beak open to her, as if expecting to be fed. The image of the creature with its beak gaping had a hallucinatory clarity. The open maw of the bird was like a small cavern, and in the cavern was a silver river, threading away into darkness. The bird made a strange cough.

Zoe stamped her foot and ran at the crows, flailing her arms. Almost grudgingly surrendering their perch, the birds dropped away from the roof of the car into clumsy, wheeling flight. From there they went gliding down into the valley, soon fading into the mist.

Zoe stared after them. She had to shake herself, almost as if to break a trance.

She remembered she'd seen a shovel stowed in the boot of the car. She took out the keys and opened the boot, found the shovel and used it to clear the snow from the windscreen, the bonnet and the rear window. Then she threw the shovel back in the boot and closed it. She went around to the front of the car and rested her weight above the airborne driver's side wheel. It rocked a little, but not too much. She tried it again, levering more weight onto it. She decided it was safe to get into the car and start it up. She thought she'd be fine so long as she didn't make any stupid mistakes with the gears.

She eased herself into the driver's seat, and waited for a moment. The car was stable. The handbrake was engaged, the gearstick rested in neutral. She slipped the key in the ignition and turned it.

The diesel engine spluttered and died. It took a few turns of the engine, but eventually it started. She gave the engine some revs, and saw through the rear-view mirror great clouds of dirty grey exhaust polluting the pure white mist behind her. Then she let the revs settle. The 4WD green light lit up the dash. She took a deep breath, engaged the clutch and slipped the car into reverse.

The back wheels spun but found no traction. She slowed the revs and tried again. This time the car eased backwards over the snow-covered rock and up across the lip of the road. She stopped the car in the middle of the road and let out a mighty breath. Trying to temper her elation, she made a three-point turn in the road and steered the car back down to the hotel.

Outside the hotel she left the engine running and the door open, and went up to get Jake. She wouldn't explain what she'd done until he came down and saw for himself.

He stood there with his arms folded and an oafish grin. 'I don't believe you did that!'

She said it wasn't difficult.

She didn't tell him about the crows.

'I don't know whether to kill you or kiss you. Can you see well enough to drive?'

'Just about.'

'You want me to drive?'

'I'm doing fine. Aren't I?'

'You are. Doing fine, you are.'

They got into the car and set off all over again.

They sat in numbed, disbelieving silence.

The police car had died on them at exactly the spot

where they'd turned around in the snowstorm earlier that morning. They could see the junction in the road. It was the same spot.

Zoe tried to turn the engine over again. The starter-motor cranked, but the engine stubbornly refused to spark.

'Let me try.'

Zoe blinked. 'What are you gonna do? Turn the key a different way?'

'Let me try it, will you?'

Zoe sighed but climbed out of the driver's seat to let Jake try his hand.

Jake had a kind of ritual in these situations. He shuffled his bottom into the seat, flexed his fingers like a concert pianist, wobbled the steering wheel, pressed down the clutch pedal and flicked the key in the ignition. Nothing. No spark. He rocked the car a little and went through his ritual all over again. Nothing. 'Is it petrol?'

'Of course it's not petrol. There's half a tank.'

'Don't get snitty. What did you do before it died on you?'

'What did I do? Nothing! I drove it, normally, standard fucking normal driving with no extra added female flourishes, okay?'

'Just be calm.'

'I didn't sing to it, or spit on the steering wheel or breathe too hard when I changed gear ... Stop making out it was something I did!'

'Well, you always screw up the DVD and the Apple Mac and the—'

'You shit!'

'Okay, you changed gear as we came up the hill?'

'No!'

'I'm just trying to establish—'

'Well, don't establish anything.'

He tried the ignition one more time. It failed again. He could almost feel the battery exhausting itself a little more every time he turned the key. 'We're on a hill, that's good. We'll bump it in reverse. I'll take the handbrake off and you give it a little push.'

Zoe went around to the front of the car. Jake engaged the clutch and put the gearstick in reverse. He nodded to her. She didn't respond. He stuck his head out of the window. 'Any time today would be, like, cool, as they say on MTV.'

She looked furious but said nothing. She compressed her lips and pushed at the front of the car. As it rolled backwards she slipped and fell on her knees. Jake let the car run for several metres before disengaging the clutch. The gears groaned and the car juddered to a halt. There was not even a cough from the engine.

He pulled on the handbrake, got out of the car and walked towards her. With the snowflakes swirling around her, settling on her hat, on her scarf, she stood in the middle of the road rubbing her skinned knees. 'Now what?'

With his back to the road leading up from the village, he stood at the T-junction and looked east and west. At least they could just about make out the road this time. There was a good chance they wouldn't fall off its edge. It was just a question of deciding which direction they should go. He took out his compass, squatted and laid it on the ground. After a few moments, he gently put it back in his pocket. 'Piece of shit!' he said softly. He was red in the face.

Zoe felt her heart squeeze for him: him with his useless compass. 'You decide.'

'No,' he said. 'You have a better sense of direction. You always have had.'

'Okay. No recriminations if I'm wrong, right? I say ... that way.'

They linked arms and set out along the road. They didn't even bother to look back at the abandoned police vehicle. It stayed at an angle in the middle of the road with the driver's door open, looking like the aftermath of a hijacking.

A little over an hour later they were back in Saint-Bernard. The familiar church tower confirmed it long before they reached the centre.

'Sorry,' Zoe said, while they were still on the road.

'No,' he said. 'Don't be. I would have picked that direction, too.'

Pretty soon Zoe had another idea. 'Follow me.'

'Seems like every time I follow you we land up in trouble.'

She ignored him, leading him back to their hotel and into the ski store: a pine-clad locker room where a giant piste map was displayed on the wall behind a sheet of Perspex. It showed that the village of Saint-Bernard nestled in a valley, with pisted ski runs flanking the village on both the north and south sides of the valley. The south side was less popular because the sun melted the snow early, but after the recent snowfall the pistes would be in good order anywhere. Zoe's plan was to get hold of some skis, ascend the south slope of the valley and ski down the other side to the neighbouring resort.

She pointed it out on the map. 'There are chairlifts right up to the top. We know the power is still on, so we can take a chairlift up. There's at least one pisted run down the other side that's marked, with a big T-bar drag lift to come back up. We're at nineteen hundred metres here, right? There's another resort over the other side at sixteen hundred metres and just a few kilometres across the mountain. There are no runs marked after the pisted one, but we can make a steady traverse. The snow's good.'

Jake breathed out. 'That might be a bit beyond our skiing abilities. You don't know what the terrain is. Rock. Trees. Deep snow. You don't know the gradient. Anything really.'

'You're a good skier. I'm a good skier.'

'Why don't we just try to walk out again? Follow the mountain road. It's much simpler.'

'Yes, we could do that. But – and it's a big but – you said yourself it's a four- or five-hour hike. We've left it too late after what just happened – we'd end up walk-ing in darkness again. If we're going to hike out of here we'll have to stay another night in the hotel and head off first thing in the morning. Or we grab some skis, get up the mountain, and from the top we could be down to that village at sixteen hundred metres in what, twenty minutes?'

'Twenty minutes? Not a chance.'

'Half an hour tops to drop down that sort of distance on skis. No more. Half an hour, Jake.'

'I don't know. I'm not happy about it. Do you think we have enough daylight left?'

'We will if we stop yakking and set off right way. Do you really want to spend another night here?'

'No.'

'Let's go for it then.'

'Look at you. You really think it's that easy, don't you?'

Zoe dusted her hands together, to show him how easy it would be.

5

They pushed open the door to a ski store and set about choosing themselves a good set of skis apiece from the rack. They told each other that they would return the skis eventually, and that no one would blame them for 'borrowing' skis, given the circumstances, though Jake joked about the growing size of their theoretical bill.

'I've always wanted some of these,' Zoe said. 'Flame orange. Top spec.'

'You would. You want new boots?'

'Sure. What about these?'

'Rack your skis up here, then, and sling me one of your boots.'

While Jake adjusted the ski bindings, Zoe poked around the shop. The owners had left in a hurry. A CD player was still switched on and there was a half-empty mug of coffee. Someone had even left a wallet under the counter. She opened it. It contained credit cards and a wad of banknotes.

She waved it at Jake. 'Look.'

'Just put it back.'

'I am putting it back. Did you think I was going to steal it?'

'I'm just saying, leave everything exactly as is. Except what we absolutely have to take.'

'Like I might do different?'

'I'm just saying.'

'Well, don't "just say". It's not like I was about to skim a few Euros from some bloke's wallet. Heck.' She put the wallet back where she found it, and then for good measure hid it under a pair of old ski gloves that were lying on the counter. 'They left really fast. I mean really, really fast.'

'That's what worries me. Here, these are done. Grab yourself a pair of fancy poles and we're away.'

They trudged through the snow carrying their new skis on their shoulders until they reached the church at the top of the hill. The streets hadn't been cleared of snow since the evacuation, so it was an easy thing to step into their bindings and slip straight down the main road, gliding through the village to the chairlifts on the south-facing slopes. Then they had to walk for a hundred metres or so to reach the lift station.

The station was utterly silent and muffled under the recent fall of snow. Even now, though the snowstorm had long subsided, a few tiny flakes still fell around them, feathering the old layers of snow covering the roof of the station shed. Jake stepped out of his bindings and pushed at the station door.

The door was stuck, frozen. He put his shoulder to it and it flew open. The air inside was still warm, as if the heating had been left running. A couple of dull green and red lights shone from a grubby console by the smeared window, alongside a shallow bank of switches. Someone had left a pack of cigarettes and a plastic lighter on the console desk.

'Do you know how to do it?' Zoe asked.

'It looks pretty much like the drag-lift equipment.

There was a nice big fat button there but I don't see one here.'

Jake went out of the station and entered the pine shed where the giant wheels and steel cables gleamed with black grease. He stared at the immobile row of sullen chairs waiting to move through the half-light on their endless loop. As he skirted the machinery he saw what he was looking for: a row of buttons and a huge emergency stop switch. He pushed the buttons hopefully but without result. When one of the buttons triggered the sound of an engine powering up and an immediate clatter of moving parts, he startled himself. The chairlift didn't move, however. The engine hummed loud in his ears as he looked for a way to send the chairs on their journey up the mountain. He saw a brake that was holding them back, and released it. Then he discovered a lever that cranked the giant overhead wheel. When the wheel began to move, so did the chairs.

Zoe had come out of the operator's cabin and was getting back into her skis. He wanted her to wait for the chairs to complete a full loop, so that they could be certain they were safe. She was less patient. Then he suggested that they take different chairs.

'Why would we do that?'

'Because,' he said calmly, 'if the lift stops and there's a healthy interval between us, at least one of us might be able to get down and do something to help the other. Whereas if we're both stuck up there, swinging in the wind, there's nothing we can do.'

'I don't see the logic. I mean, if we both happen to get off at the end just as the lift stops, then we're in a better position than if one is safely off and one is stuck up in the air.'

'That's ridiculous.'

'No more ridiculous than your idea. It's just random luck. Random together or random separate. We're still subject to randomness. I'd rather we face that random together.'

There and then, in the deserted ski village, with the chairlift engine whistling over their heads and the empty, icy, snow-covered chairs proceeding up the snowy mountain one by one, they had an argument about randomness.

'After everything that's happened to us, I'd rather we climbed in the same chair,' Zoe said. 'For fuck's sake, I can't believe we're arguing about this!'

Jake sighed and shuffled along to form up with his skis. They stood side by side waiting for the next six-man chair to come around, and as soon as it bunted the backs of their knees they dropped into position. Jake reached for the safety bar and pulled it down.

They ascended the slope in silence.

It was a long chairlift, and secretly both were wondering what they would do exactly if the chair *did* stop. For much of the journey they were fifteen metres off the ground. The cable mechanism thrummed steadily and the wind manufactured ghost-like whistles and moans around the pylons at regular intervals. The returning chairs on the other side of the pylons, having been exposed on the mountainside without service, were piled with snow and hung with ice; grim dark chariots, it seemed to Zoe, returning after depositing their cargoes in a place of death.

As they made their ascent, below them the build-up of snow on the branch of a pine would reach its limit and trigger a sudden spray of snow. Other than that there was no movement anywhere.

'So quiet,' Zoe said, if only to resist the baleful murmur of the wind in the pylons.

The chair juddered as it approached the penultimate pylon and tilted into its descent. Jake lifted back the safety bar. They shuffled their bottoms in the chair, readying their skis to glide off at the lift terminal. When they did so they hit deep snow and came to an abrupt stop. Normally the dismount point was packed and maintained by lift operators.

'The piste is going to be deep,' Jake said.

'We'll take it steady. Are you going to shut off the lift?'

'I'll leave it running.'

'Why?'

'Why? Why? Why? Are you going to contradict everything I say?' At least he was smiling about it now. 'Why do I get a whole lifetime of why why why?

'It just seems … a waste of energy. We should shut it off.'

'I want it to stay running. I want people to know we're here, okay? Stop trying to be top banana about everything, will you?'

'You're the one who does top banana.'

'Listen to that! That's such a top-banana statement. Can't you see that?'

'Can we just look at the map, please?'

Jake shuffled across to where Zoe was studying her map.

'It's not difficult,' she said without looking up. 'We go halfway down the piste, then cut off on this track through the woods. After a while we should meet a winding road – probably a lumber track – through the forest and we can follow it all the way to the next village. There won't be any traffic to worry about.'

Jake fixed the retaining straps of his ski poles over his wrists.

'Wait,' Zoe said. 'Take a moment to look at this, Jake. People would pay a king's ransom to be here on virgin snow with no one else about. In fact you couldn't buy it. No one can. Look: it's so beautiful.'

Jake snorted. Here they were trying to get out of the place with their lives, but she was right. There wasn't a track anywhere to be seen in the light, powdery snow. The grey, pregnant clouds loured above them, but there were blue smudges in the sky. A transforming power had breathed over the land and turned it into a perfect wedding cake, and the two of them were now perched on the top like a marzipan bride and groom.

'Kiss me,' Zoe said.

His lips were cold but she wanted to thaw them with her kiss. She didn't want to pull away, but eventually Jake did. She blinked at him. For a moment she thought she saw something strange reflected in the black glass of his pupils.

'What?'

'Nothing. Come on. It's a black slope but it doesn't look too steep,' she said. 'Just make sure you don't miss the turn.'

'Sounds like I'm following you again. Fucking banana-face.'

They plunged across the slope, and the snow was thick and crusty on the unprepared piste, but it represented no challenge to their abilities. Their skis ran a little slower, but the snow peeled away from the blades of their skis with a soft, sensual whisper. It was possible, on the deserted slope, to make wide, wheeling, swooping turns and leave perfect parallel tracks behind. Within a couple of minutes they were already halfway down the run. Zoe had drawn up at the side of the piste.

Jake came gliding to a stop beside her.

'Enjoy that?' she asked.

'Oh yessir.'

'That was the easy bit. Now we have to drop through here.'

A clearing in the trees at the side of the piste led to a thickly wooded and more steeply plunging descent. Outcrops of sharp limestone rock stuck up through the snow. Though they were both experienced skiers, neither of them had done more than short-burst or open-mountain off-piste skiing. This was going to be something new.

Reading his apprehension, she said, 'We just ski where we can, side-slip where can't, step round, or take off our skis and walk where we have to. Ready?'

She didn't wait for his answer. She turned her skis towards the trees and let them glide into the mouth of the dark woods.

Ten minutes later they were in trouble. The terrain was steep and uneven. Jagged teeth of amber rock broke through the snow at random intervals; the pine trees hid aggressive roots under the deceptively smooth white carpet and thrust stout, low-hanging branches at shoulder height above it. Finding a path between the trunks was tricky. The going was made worse by the presence of semi-frozen channels carrying meltwater down the mountain. Some of these streams were hidden by snow bridges; others were open and too wide to step across. They lost a lot of time trying to negotiate these streams, and sometimes had to step back uphill when it became impossible to simply point the skis down the fall-line.

Zoe fell early and took a crack on her arm from a boulder. Jake also went on his back twice when his skis got tangled in black roots or hidden snares under the snow. He shed a ski and they lost a lot of time finding it and digging it out. They pressed on, helping each other where they could. They tried to take off their skis and carry them on their shoulders; but in their heavy moulded boots they were plunging thigh-deep into snow at times, so they abandoned that idea.

Opportunities to let the skis run never delivered them more than fifteen or twenty metres. It took them two hours to make the kind of distance they had covered on the piste in two or three minutes.

They made a stop, cleared a space in the snow and rested. Though both knew that the light was fading. They could not be caught in the woods on skis after dark.

'I didn't think it would be quite as tricky as this,' Zoe said.

'How much further, would you guess?'

'So long as we keep heading downhill at an angle, we have to hit that road through the woods. Can't be above an hour. Or two at the rate we're going.'

'An hour or two until we get to the next village? Or an hour or two until we hit the road?'

'One or the other.'

They sat in the profound silence of the snow and the woods. She wished he would say something.

'I'm sorry for bringing you this way,' she said. 'You can give me hell if you like.'

'It was a good idea.'

'No it wasn't.'

'It was a brave idea, at any rate.'

She wished he would tease her. When they had no banter, that meant the situation was serious. Zoe looked through the trees up at the grey sky. She hoped the thinning light would hold out long enough for them.

'Ready to go again?'

'Ready.'

In fact they met the road just half an hour after they'd got started again. It was no more than a logging track winding between the trees, but it plunged downwards and Zoe was elated because her map-reading had been accurate. It had been tricky, but they'd made it.

It was a huge relief to ski freely again. The road was deep with snow and a little narrow but it presented no further challenge to their skiing abilities. The light around them was fading rapidly now. On occasion the road would hit a dip and if they couldn't generate enough momentum to carry them up the other side they had to sidestep up; but that exertion was invariably rewarded with a free sweep through the dusk downwards on the other side.

Eventually the spruce and the fir parted wide enough to afford them a glimpse of lights twinkling in the small village below. As they got nearer they could see illuminated hotels and houses, and cars parked alongside the road leading into the village.

They hugged and laughed, and confessed that back up in the woods they'd both been too afraid to admit that they had been out of their depth. But now they

73

could let their skis glide further down the track, a little more slowly, though, for fear of encountering moving traffic.

But there was no moving traffic. And as they entered the village there was no sign of people, either. It was as deserted as the village they had left behind them.

Jake spoke first. 'You're not going to like this.'

'What?'

'I think they've evacuated this place, too.'

Zoe groaned.

They had arrived at a flat stretch of road and had to take off their skis and carry them over their shoulders. They marched into the centre of the deserted village, scanning the houses for the least sign of activity, like soldiers in a conflict but carrying skis instead of guns.

Zoe's face clouded over. 'This can't be right. This just can't be right.'

'What?'

'Stop. Stop. Look at that hotel. And look at the church at the top of the hill.'

'What about it?'

'The tower. It's the same. Same as the one in our village.'

'Similar.'

'Not similar, Jake. Not similar at all. It's the same. So is that hotel. We're back in Saint-Bernard. We haven't gone anywhere!'

Jake half-smiled at her, an agonised grin of disbelief. He looked up the road, squinting at the church ahead. Then behind him, to examine the road they'd come in on. He twisted his neck around all points of the compass. Finally he threw down his skis and poles in a clatter and went running, in his heavy ski boots, up the hill towards the church.

Zoe was right. It was the same church. Same hotel. Same houses and streets. Same supermarket, with the police station next to it.

They'd circled back on themselves.

Jake ripped his woollen hat from his head and ran his fingers through the sweaty strands of his hair. Then he walked back down to Zoe. She was crouching, holding her gloved fists under her nose, looking up at him. 'How?' he wanted to know.

'It's not possible.'

'We must have taken a wrong turn.' He couldn't keep the blame out of his voice. She'd been leading, after all.

'It's just not possible.'

'Of course it's possible. We've just proved it's fucking possible. Here we are. Q. E. Fucking. D.'

'No. You're wrong. We went up that mountain, and on that side.'

'There must be a pass! A pass must snake through the mountain and wind back down here. We've inadvertently followed a pass.'

'I'm sorry, Jake! I'm really sorry!'

He looked like he wanted to be furious with her, but he couldn't. He'd asked her to go in front, after all. He had no sense of direction whatsoever himself, and he had been the one who'd told her to lead the way.

'Fuuuuuuuuuuuuuuuucccccccccccccccckkkkkkkkk! It's a joke! I feel like someone is having a laugh!'

'Jake!'

The road delivered them to the opposite side of the village, in the same place where they'd emerged when they'd tried to walk out. They had to walk past the church all over again. Jake took his compass out of his pocket and in frustration he hurled it at the silver tower of the church.

'Don't do that.'

'Where you going?'

Zoe walked up to the door of the church and pushed it open. In the traditional Catholic style it was a cave of shadows and echoes and images of agony, relieved by alcoves in which numerous candles were burning. Jake entered the church behind her. Their footsteps echoed on the stone flags. The air inside the church was cold. Their breath was visible.

'It's almost like something is keeping us here in this village,' Zoe said, looking around her and up at the ceiling. 'Like something doesn't want to let us go.'

'I feel the same thing. I felt it before today. I just didn't want to say it.' Jake glanced around the vaulted ceiling of the church, and at its walls and doors, as if looking for something that might sign them a way out, or offer them a clue, but there was nothing. He stared for a while at the steadily burning candles.

'Come on.'

Jake looked exhausted, so Zoe marshalled him back to the hotel and immediately ran him a hot bath. She found the storeroom and raided it for bath foam and fresh towels. She thought he was worn out with anxiety. She knew he felt acutely his masculine duty to get them out of this situation, and that he was failing; even though she wasn't the sort of woman to need that; even though she accepted responsibility as much as he did. It was a weakness in him, something his father had taught him, a controlling thing. A protective instinct, for which she could easily forgive him. But nature didn't seem to be playing by the rules and it was wearing him out.

After his bath she helped dry him and bullied him into bed. Within minutes he'd fallen asleep.

She sat watching him sleep. It was impossible to stop loving Jake. He was so full of fire and fight and goodness, and yet so vulnerable when he was tired. They'd been together for more than ten years, and in all that time she'd kept an inextinguishable candle burning for him. She decided that thought was both trite and not. It had occurred to her when she'd seen the candles burning brightly in the church of Saint Bernard.

Something about the church, and the candles in particular, bothered her greatly.

She wondered who had lit the candles in the church.

Though she didn't know anything about it, she assumed that candles – even good quality church or otherwise candles – didn't burn for days on end. She therefore assumed someone had to keep them going: that it was a job of work for some church acolyte.

She stood over Jake, listening to his breathing, making sure he was deeply asleep. Then she let herself out of the room, closing the door behind her with a soft click. She rode the elevator down to the lobby and walked from there into the restaurant.

She went directly to the table at which they'd had dinner and drunk champagne the previous evening. The plates and glasses and remains of their meal were all exactly as they had left them when Zoe had wantonly dragged him off to bed. And in the middle of the table, a candle – a candle that she herself had lit – was burning.

Still.

She clearly remembered lighting that candle. It had

been a new candle, with a fresh white wick. That meant that it had burned all evening, and all night, and all day, too, while they'd been out. It just hadn't burned down. Not a centimetre. Not half a centimetre. There was no sign of wax having dripped from the flame. It could have been lit just a moment ago.

She blew at the candle and the flame snuffed out, with a smell of wax and a twist of grey smoke released into the air. Then she lit it again, and the flame burned brightly.

From there she went into the kitchen. Some of the unwashed pots and pans, left behind after Jake's cooking adventures the previous evening, lay carelessly discarded. But on another side of the kitchen, on a clean worktop, lay the meat and chopped vegetables that had rested there untouched since they'd walked into the kitchen on the afternoon of the avalanche.

She made a close inspection. The rosy meat, tinted with delicate marble-threads of white fat, glistened as if it had been chopped only moments earlier. The vegetables too exhibited a healthy, freshly sliced hue. Neither the meat nor the vegetables showed the slightest signs of decomposition.

She had to think hard, once again, to work out exactly how long it had been since they were caught in the avalanche. Oddly enough it felt as though they had been living in that place for weeks; but this was only the third day. But that meant that the meat and vegetables had sat on the worktop for between fifty and sixty hours in this warm kitchen. She picked up a strip of meat and sniffed it. It smelled perfectly fresh. She bit into a crisp slice of carrot. She lifted a slice of celery to her nose. It smelled garden-fresh, beautiful. It was showing no sign of wilt. She snapped the celery in half and it broke cleanly, and with a click.

Candles that didn't burn. Meat that didn't decompose. Vegetables that didn't wilt. She stared at the meat on the worktop slab for a long time.

A hand touched her on the shoulder from behind. She screamed.

It was Jake. He wore his bath robe.

'Don't do that!'

'I've had the very same thoughts,' he said. 'The candles. The food. I looked at it last night. I just didn't want to say.'

'But what does it mean?'

Jake turned away and sorted through some kitchen implements. He found a very sharp chopping knife. He waved the knife at her, then rolled up his sleeve.

'What are you doing, Jake?'

With his eyes trained on hers he sliced the inside of his forearm, making a gash a couple of centimetres wide. The flesh opened up and he winced at the pain. But no blood flowed. Not a single drop.

'Jake! Stop it!'

He made another smaller incision on the tip of his ring finger on his left hand. Again he winced at the bite of the knife, but again there was no flow of blood, not even a pinprick. He put down the kitchen knife, rolled down his sleeve. 'I cut myself while I was cooking and playing the fool last night. It was a deep cut. But no blood. I decided not to tell you. God. I love you, Zoe.'

His eyes were misted.

She blinked at him. 'I love you too, Jake. Please tell me what's going on.'

'You don't know what this means?'

'No! Please tell me! And please stop harming your-self, my love!'

'It means we died,' said Jake.

6

The snow stopped. The swollen grey clouds drifted on and the sun appeared in the ice-blue sky. The sun lanced off the snow and they had to wear sunglasses all the time. Good sunglasses, expensive ones, and all they had to do was walk into a store and pick out the very best designer pairs available.

Of course Zoe did not immediately accept that they had died in the avalanche. Swallowing that was more than a little difficult.

For who could acknowledge such a thing? But it was as if once Jake had enunciated the fact, and had himself accepted the logic of the situation and openly proclaimed it, then the weather had changed accordingly. There was no longer any need – it seemed – for the world to be wrapped in a spectral mist of snow, and the best of all possible worlds could be on display.

Naturally Zoe blanked the idea. She insisted they walk out of the village all over again, this time on the clear roads. Jake offered no resistance, beyond commenting that it would make no difference. He was right: even on a clear day, with no confusion over the direction in which they walked, the roads unaccountably delivered them back to Saint-Bernard-en-Haut all over again. They commandeered the police car again and successfully started it up; but whichever route they drove it was as if a giant, gentle hand curved the road and steered them back to their starting point.

'How can this be?' she had railed. 'How can this be happening?'

Jake had merely blinked his eggshell-blue eyes. 'I've explained it to you. There's no more to be said.'

Four days of this. It was impossible; it couldn't be happening; it made no sense; it defied natural law. But there it was. And in that time lighted candles did not burn down, meat and vegetables on the slab showed no sign of decay or wilt, and blood did not flow.

While her brain resisted and reasoned, fought and tested the uncanny and undeniable logic, her heart never accepted any of it.

'I can't be dead. I can feel pain. I can feel pleasure.'

'I know. I know.'

'I know I love you. That can't be death, can it?'

'I'm not saying I understand it.'

'It's not hell to be here. It's not heaven either, because I keep thinking the avalanche is going to come down over us.'

'The avalanche already came down, my darling. That's what you won't accept. We died in the avalanche.'

'No, I mean the bigger one. There's a big avalanche up there, waiting. I can feel it. I can feel the tension in the air. Maybe this sunshine is going to melt the snow and bring it crashing down. Do you think it's like this for everyone?'

They sat on the snow-carpeted steps of the village church, stunned, exhausted and bewildered by the compact nature of their new existence.

Jake took off his sunglasses and thumbed his still-bloodshot eyes. Zoe kept asking him questions, as if he knew, as if he had the faintest idea of the answers. If this were an afterlife, would it last for ever? Did it fade? Would other people come into it? Could they die inside this death? Why was time there measured by the movement of the sun and the moon but not by the burning of a candle? She had a hundred such questions, and Jake would say: *All I know is that there is sun and sky and snow and me and you, that's all I know*. And she would rage against him, until he felt obliged to try to answer the questions for her, even though he admitted now that he'd spent all of his life pretending to know the unknowable, pretending to be able to outstare the man in the hood.

'What man in the hood?'

'The one who watches us all.'

'You mean Death? Is that what you mean?'

If Jake was right, Zoe thought, and they had died in the avalanche then all the great religions of the world were wrong, that much was clear. The sacred building right behind them was a cold shell, populated by flickering points of hope, and no more than that. Only one question remained: what were they to do? What to do?

'Tell me,' he said. 'Have you actually felt cold? Since it happened, I mean. Since the day of the avalanche?'

'I don't know.'

'Believe it or not, it was only three days ago, no ... four days.'

'Was it? It feels like ... much longer. Much longer.'

'Weeks, yes. But it isn't. And my point is, have you actually felt cold? You see, we've been sitting here an hour. And I don't feel cold at all.'

'Take your clothes off,' she said. 'You'll feel cold pretty quick.'

So he did. He shrugged his ski jacket off, and his pullover. Then he took off his boots and his salopettes, and then he stripped off his thermal underwear and his thick socks. Naked, he lowered his bare bottom onto the snowy step.

She watched his eyes, waiting. He held her gaze.

I'm not going to say anything, she thought. *If he wants to play games …*

But several minutes went by. Maybe ten, maybe fifteen. No, maybe two minutes.

'Admit it,' she said at last. 'You're fucking freezing.'

He shook his head, no.

Zoe stood up, pulled off her jacket and unbuckled her trouser belt. She undressed completely and sat beside him, her bare bottom on the icy snow. She linked her arm through his and leaned her head on his shoulder. 'You know what? Even if we don't need clothes I'm not going around naked.'

'Me neither.'

'Maybe I would if this were a tropical island.'

'But it's not.'

'Do you think that the place where everyone dies is where they get to be afterwards? I mean, if you'd died in the trenches of the First World War, are you stuck there for eternity?'

'Who says we're here for eternity?' he said. 'My arse should be blue. I can't feel the cold at all. Can you remember what it was like?'

Zoe thought hard. 'Remember it for me.'

Jake said, 'It was like catching a finger under a hammer. It was like a burn. It was like a mouth, sucking at you, stinging as it sucked. It was like a knife sharpening itself on you, whetting itself so it could cut you.'

She winced. 'My God, I am fucking freezing! Look – I'm shivering!' She jumped up and started pulling her clothes back on. Her teeth chattered. 'I don't know if I just remembered it or if I felt it, but I'm going to put my clothes back on. Aren't you cold?'

He shrugged. 'I'll get dressed. Shall we go back to the hotel?'

Zoe was now perishing as she waited for Jake to put his clothes back on. With the winter sunlight dipping over the mountain, and with their shadows flung before them across the white snow, they walked back together. As they passed some shops, Zoe peeled away from him. 'I'll catch up. I want to pick up some things.'

'I'll come with you.'

'It's okay. I'll catch up.'

'I'll wait.'

'Jake, are you afraid we'll lose each other? I just want to pick up some things.'

'What things?'

'Some more eye-drop from the pharmacy, stuff like that. I'll be two minutes!'

He shook his head and walked on.

Zoe pushed open the door to the pharmacy. The lights were on, as they always had been. She knew where to go to get the eye-drops because she'd picked them up on that first day. But that wasn't what she'd come for. There was something else.

'I'm not dead,' she said, as she moved between the aisles of the pharmacy. 'I'm not dead.'

'What do you want to eat tonight?' Jake said when she came into the hotel room. 'What do dead people eat?'

'Don't.'

85

'Well, we have to eat something.'

'Do we? Do you actually feel hungry? Have you actually felt hunger these last few days? Or are we just eating because it's what we do?'

Jake opened his mouth to speak but then closed it. He had to think about it. She pushed past him to get into the bathroom and closed the door behind her.

She opened the small carton and unwrapped the plastic stick from its foil packet. She dropped her trousers and pants, holding the stick under her as she tried to piss on the half-centimetre by three-centimetre absorbent stick without pissing on her hand. At first she couldn't seem to pee at all. It was as if she'd forgotten how. Then she didn't seem to want to stop. In any event, she'd covered the stick for more than the required five seconds. She replaced the cap on the stick, sat on the toilet and waited.

After about a minute Jake thumped on the door.

'Can't I use the toilet in peace, Jake!'

She heard some muttering

'For God's sake, there's a corridor full of rooms, each with its own toilet. Go and find your own.'

She heard more muttering, and the outer door opened and closed.

When she examined the stick, there were two clear blue lines. There was no question that she was still pregnant.

Jake knew nothing of this. It was the sixty-four-million-dollar question she'd been waiting to ask him and she'd been looking for a suitable moment. The moment when the stars aligned.

For all of the time they had been together neither of them had been much interested in having children.

Then her feelings started to change. The thing was, she wanted Jake's feelings to change along with hers, to mesh, to cog; and she suspected that was going to be unlikely. They had discussed it once or twice, and the question had evaporated. There wasn't a no. But there wasn't a yes in the air, either.

They had watched with rotating envy, suspicion and horror as friends of theirs became parents. They had seen lives changed, both for better and for worse. In some cases the advent of parenthood had been a thrilling and giddy elevation of life into the upper air; in others it had been a chaotic nosedive into disaster and divorce. For some, becoming a mother or a father channelled a blissed-out source of energy and joy; others were exhausted drones, depressed and zoned out by the experience. There seemed to be no rules for how the thing played itself out in people's lives.

But when she had fallen pregnant just before their skiing holiday, Zoe knew she wanted it. She was just not the sort of woman to drag a man kicking and screaming into fatherhood. Her plan had been to await the magical moment, perhaps at the top of a mountain or during a walk through the perfect snow of early evening, and with dusk settling to sound him out; and if the auguries were positive, she would reveal her sensational news.

But then the avalanche.

And now, although every sinew and nerve inside her resisted the premise, she was dead.

Pregnant and dead.

The new question of course concerned the nature of her pregnancy. Was it the kind of pregnancy that gestated and changed with the passing of the sun across the sky; or one that remained in a state of stasis, a frozen embryo suspended inside her, like the candle flame that never progressed down the wax? If it were the former would she tell Jake? And would she if it were the latter? Perhaps if they were trapped here for eternity, she would be eternally pregnant, without ever arriving at full term.

She heard the outer door open and close as Jake came back into the room. She hoiked up her trousers, flushed the toilet and carefully hid the tester stick at the bottom of the bathroom bin. When she emerged Jake was leaning against the wall with his arms folded, looking at her strangely.

'When did you last have a dump?'

'What?'

'When? Because I didn't have a dump since the avalanche until just now. And the urge only came on me when you mentioned being hungry. I thought about that and felt hungry. That made me remember that I hadn't had a dump. And remembering not having a dump before made me suddenly have to go for a dump.'

'Jake, do you think we're trapped here? Or have we been released here?'

'You think about it hard enough and you'll want a dump too.'

'Can you shut up about dumping?'

'Just sayin', okay?'

'It's an important question – if we're trapped, or if we've been freed to be here. It will change the way we are when we're here, won't it?'

'We're at cross-purposes, aren't we? Talking on different levels.'

'You could say that.'

'Dumping is a very important question.'

'Hell! I suppose I haven't since the avalanche. It's probably the trauma. You know? A reaction. Now I've started thinking about, I have to go.'

'That's what I mean,' he said.

She turned and went back into the bathroom, shutting the door on him.

'It's always good,' Jake shouted through the closed door, 'to take a happy dump.'

'Shut up!'

Jake moved away from the door. 'Always good to take a happy dump,' he said quietly.

In the night she was awoken by a bright white disc hovering in the air close to her face. A voice clearly whispered her name:

'Zoe! Zoe! Approach the light! Come into the light.'

Zoe sat up in bed, squinting between her splayed fingers at the source of the light. 'You know what?' she said. 'Even as a dead person you can be such an arsehole.'

Jake switched off the lamp he was holding a few centimetres away from Zoe's face and put it back on the bedside table. 'I couldn't sleep. I keep thinking about our situation.'

A crack of light leaked through the curtains. Zoe got up and drew back the curtains and the room was washed by thrilling moonlight. Outside it reflected brilliantly on the snow. It was enough to see by. 'Pour us both a cognac. Let's talk.'

Jake splashed the amber liquid into a pair of tumblers, handing one of them to Zoe. He took a drink and sniffed.

'I want to ask you something,' she said. 'It was something I asked you yesterday, but I want you to think hard about it before answering.'

'Fire away.' He took another sip. 'You know what? This cognac doesn't taste of cognac.'

'I asked you if you thought we're trapped here, or if we've been freed here.'

'Depends which way you choose to see it.'

'Exactly. There isn't a right answer, is there? It depends on how we choose to see it. If we choose to see it as if we're trapped here, then our situation is tragic. If we choose to see that we've been liberated here, then it's the opposite.'

'Comic?'

'Comic isn't the opposite of tragic.'

'No.'

'I mean to say, if we choose to see it the right way, we could have the most magical time here. You and me. Together and alone. We have warmth, shelter, food, the best wine, skiing on wonderful slopes together. It's paradise: if we choose to accept it. If we choose to call it that.'

'I guess.'

'You guess?'

'Well, yes. You could be right.'

She heard the shadow on his words. 'But. There's a but, isn't there? There's always a but.'

'No, you're right. We can be free, together, staying here, playing in the snow like children, with all our needs taken care of.'

'But. Tell me your but.'

'Okay. It's like this. Even though there is no decay here, even though meat stays fresh and candles don't burn down, there is still another level in which time is passing. The sun goes down and comes up. We sleep, we pee, we dump. There is energy, keeping the lights on, driving the chairlifts. And energy burning is an event. And the event must pass.'

'I don't know what you're getting at.'

'Been thinking about it. In all our folklore about death, someone comes to collect us. You know, Uncle Derek in a surgical gown telling you to go into the light. The Devil shovelling you into his furnace. Charon to row you across the River Styx. I can't help feeling someone or something ... is coming.'

'Coming?'

'Yes ... coming. To collect us.'

Zoe shivered. 'I wish you hadn't said that.'

He went over to the window and looked out across the lustrous moonlit snow. 'Me too. I also wish I hadn't said it. But ... that's my but about all this. I feel it. I feel something coming.'

'You don't believe in any of that! Charon, the Devil, Uncle Derek! Maybe this is an atheist's afterlife. You're an atheist to the bone, like I am.'

'I am. And I'm not backing away from that. I just feel that someone or something is making its way here.' He drained his glass. 'What does this cognac taste like to you?'

They went out to ski. Zoe said that she'd come to this place to ski and that she wanted to ski, so out they went. She asked if they might try the same route by which they'd tried to leave the village after the avalanche. Jake knew that she was going to want to cut through the trees all over again, to find a way out, but he said nothing. He seemed resigned to letting her try, as if he knew what was going to happen. It made no difference if they tried or if they didn't.

The chairlift running up the south side of the valley was still in motion, exactly as they had left it. The engine emitted a low hum and machinery rattled as empty chairs were whisked around at the bottom of the lift and sent back up in pointless ascent; on the other side the chairs returned in regular order, somehow looking as if they'd been through fire; or through a war; or had survived some bitter experience that, regardless, had left them stoic and unmoved. Though they were just empty chairs, there was a horrible futility in the repetition of their tracked existence along the cable lines. As if they'd had the chance to learn something, but failed.

They dropped into a chair together. Jake put his arm around Zoe. She let herself snuggle into him as they were whisked above the trees. She saw him scanning the white wilderness below.

'What are you looking for?' she asked.

'Tracks.'

'Tracks of what?'

'Anything alive. Fox. Hare. Chamois. Pine martens. Anything. Bird tracks even.' He leaned across the chair, scanning the pristine snow between the trees. 'I haven't seen a living thing since the day of the avalanche.'

'I have.'

'Really.'

'There were two crows.'

'Really?'

'I haven't seen them since.' She fell silent, thinking about the crows. There was only the hum of the cable, and a chatter as the chair rode over a pylon, followed by a regular flapping of the cable like large leathery wings. Then there was quiet again, with only the sob of the wind in the taut wires.

'What does it mean?' she asked.

'What?'

'The crows.'

'I don't know. I don't know that it means anything. It was just two crows. Does everything have to mean something?'

There was no answer to this, other than the chatter of the chair. At the top of the lift they easily glided off. Jake re-fixed his hat and threaded his pole straps over his wrists.

'It's beautiful. It's so beautiful. Jake, Can we—'

'Yes.'

'Yes to what? You don't know what I'm going to ask.'

'Halfway down. Can we turn off into the woods. Try again. Yes.'

'I made such a bad job of skiing it the other day. I only want to see if I can do it better.'

He smiled. 'That's a good reason.'

'We can be a little more relaxed this time.'

'Sure. We'll stop at the same place.'

Jake pushed off, letting the skis glide. The quality of the snow had changed. It was still deep and unblemished, unpisted by machines, but the sun had softened it and the skis ran fractionally slower, and with more of a hiss.

Zoe came behind him. The sky was an astonishing blue and the larch and pine mingled with spruce wove a thrilling flank of green velvet either side of the waxen white slope. Zoe knew that just to let the skis run was the nearest she could ever come to flying.

I am falling through the rings of heaven.

The virgin snow parted for the floating tips of her skis. Way, way down the slope she looked back to see Jake, in his black ski suit, swooping down the run like a beautiful crow, offering barely a turn, wheeling only when he approached Zoe so that he could draw up beside her.

'I didn't know I'd passed you,' she said.

'You were in your own world.'

'I was. Just for a minute I was a bird. So were you.'

'Through the trees now?'

'Through the trees.'

They managed it more effectively this time, and where they didn't, they laughed, and their shared laughter cut through the silent trees. It was a little like laughing in church: whether it was approved of or frowned upon depended on the aspect of your God. They sprang across icy streams, and stepped around outcrops of stone that resembled the half-buried fists or knuckled fingers of giants. They slipped between the shadowy spruce and pine, triggering flurries and falls of powder behind them.

It was difficult going, but they got through it without taking a fall this time before hitting the same snow-covered logging road. They knew it would carry them back into Saint-Bernard, so without a word, they plunged further down through the trees, only to find another loop of the road beneath them, and a steep edge they couldn't cross. Surrendering again to the inevitable, they let the skis ride the logging road back into the village.

There were no signs of the ski tracks they had made on their first attempt to abandon the village. All had been covered over. Jake stopped twice on the way down, turning to look back. He said he thought there might be someone or something behind him, following them. Or maybe he just wanted there to be something behind him.

They saw nothing. A kind of acceptance came over them.

They set chairlifts and drag lifts running all over the village, opening up a network of runs. The snow conditions were perfect. The sky was the blue of a prayer and the sun made it possible for them to leave off their coats.

'I'm skiing better than I've ever done,' Zoe said.

'Me too. You want to stop for lunch?'

'I'm not hungry.'

'Me neither, but I want to stop at one of these mountain restaurants, build a fire and relax in front of it.'

'Are you cold?'

'Not at all. But it's what I want to do. We eat when we're not hungry; drink when we're not thirsty; and I want to relax when I'm not tired.'

'Okay. I'll race you to La Chamade.' She was already sweeping down the fall-line.

Zoe stood at the entrance to the mountain restaurant, skis off, holding them upright, waiting. 'Slacker.'

'I don't know how you do it.'

There were a couple of abandoned ski sets, ice-packed and snow-covered, resting against the rack outside the log-built restaurant. They set their skis upright on the rack next to them and went inside. The lights were on in the kitchen but not the dining room. La Chamade had a large open stone hearth, with a ready basket of logs. Jake went into the back to find kindling and matches, then quickly made up the fire. The pine logs spat as they caught.

He sniffed at the smoke. 'Can you smell the pine logs?'

'Yes. Or maybe I can now you've said it.'

'Can you remember that feeling, of coming in from the cold snow, maybe when your fingers and your toes are aching from the chill of it, and you sit near a fire and your cheeks start to flame, and the pleasure of thawing out, and what it does to your blood?'

She shuffled over to him and leaned her head on his shoulder. 'I can remember. I'm feeling it now.'

'That's just it, isn't it? We remember it, and then we feel it. You describe the sensation to me and then I feel it. But not before the fact. Not before.'

Zoe started to cry. 'Where are we? What's happening?'

'Come here. Don't cry now. I don't know the answer. I only know one thing: to be here alone, to be experiencing this on my own, that would be hell. With you here, I can do it.'

She hugged him and looked at him. 'I'm not unhappy. I'm bewildered, and more than a bit scared.'

'But do you understand, Zoe? We have to remember things for each other. This life, whatever it is, we re-make for each other.'

'I think I understand.'

He went to the bar, found a bottle of red wine and removed the cork. He brought the bottle and two glasses, filling one for each of them. 'Taste it.' He read the label. 'It's an Albert Bichot Gevrey-Chambertin les Corvées 2004 Burgundy, which means bugger-all to me, so I don't know if it's good or bad, if it costs an arm and a leg or if it's a cheap one. You're on your own. Tell me what you think.'

She stuck her nose in the glass first, like a connoisseur. Then she tasted, holding the wine on her tongue for a moment before letting it wash around her mouth. She thought about sugar and acidity and tannin, then about fruit and spice and earthiness. Then she swallowed it, thinking about whether she truly wanted another sip, or not.

He looked at her expectantly with his still-bloodshot eyes.

'You want me to be honest? It doesn't taste of anything. Neutral.'

'Exactly. Like everything around here. But what if I remember for you how good red wine tastes. That it has the savour of, maybe, cherries, but a bit spicy. That it's a bit woody, like oak, and that there are all kinds of savoury tensions on your tongue, sweet and acid, dry and fluid. And that the taste persists, light, but a pleasant aftertaste.'

'I can taste all that now!'

'And doesn't it evoke the cardinal's red robe and the Devil's furnace?'

'Now you're talking bollocks. Although, now you come to mention it ...'

'Sin and redemption?'

'Honey and fire?'

'You're going to have to pour me another glass. Does it still taste of nothing to you?'

'No – it tastes of all the things you say, it really does.

It really, really does. Don't you think that's odd?

'Everything is odd here.'

'No, I mean the way it only tastes of something after we've talked about it. And I had no idea you knew so much about wine.'

'I don't. I was making it up. At least I think I was. The point is that here, we can tell our own story. The story of what happens. We don't have to let other people tell us the story and— Did you hear that?'

'Hear what?'

Jake was on his feet and striding across to the window. 'I swear I heard a dog bark.'

'A dog?'

'Yes, a dog. I heard it bark. Really clear, with an echo across the snow.'

She joined him at the window. 'I didn't hear anything.'

'I wasn't imagining it.'

'I'm not saying you did.'

'I know you're not saying I did. When I say I'm not imagining things, I'm talking to myself.'

'I can't see anything out there.'

'There was a dog. Or at least there was a bark. I'm going out to look.'

She shrugged and let him go and she sat by the fire and waited. She took another sip of the cardinal's red robe. The fire burned in the hearth without a crackle: clean, orange flames, like fingers reaching from under the curve of the log, cradling it, almost lovingly, as it burned. She turned from the fire, looked out, and saw Jake trudging through the snow.

After a while he came back. 'Nothing,' he said in a depressed voice.

'Well.'

'I could have sworn.'

'Drink some more wine.'

They finished off the bottle of red wine. Now it tasted of many wonderful things.

'It would be good,' he said.

'What would?'

'If there was a dog.'

She held his hand in hers. 'Do you think we'll ever get over that? The sadness? The regret?'

He drained his glass and placed it on the table. 'Let's go and have some fun.'

They went up the drag lift onto a long easy run and skied down backwards together all the way. They took a steep red run and came down carving precision turns, she trying to keep in his tracks exactly, and then reversing the order. They found their way into the snowboarding park and rode a few jumps. Their skiing seemed to have improved disproportionately to the time they had spent on the skis. Zoe said skiers always remember themselves as performing better than they had in reality; Jake agreed but said he could never remember being *this* good. The skiing was by no means effortless, but their technical proficiency was a surprise to both of them.

The snowboard park had a control station with a sound system for broadcasting through speakers wired across the slopes. Jake found a Jimi Hendrix CD, cranked up the volume and they spent the rest of the afternoon tearing around the snowboard park, running the half-pipes and quarter-pipes, leaping the spines and tabletops. They'd both started out as snowboarders but had moved over to skis in favour of speed.

After a couple of hours the light started to fade. Jake wanted to leave the music running, but Zoe made him turn it off. She said she liked to hear the sound of the moon and the stars over the snow and it seemed so right at the time that he didn't question it. They let their skis glide them back to their hotel.

As they arrived at the bottom of the slope, a dog barked, clearly in the cold. The bark seemed to hang in the icy air.

'I heard it that time, Jake!'

'Over there. Near the trees.'

'There it is!'

At the foot of the ski slope was a thin clump of trees dividing two nursery runs. A medium-sized black dog sat back on its haunches, muzzle pointing up, its front paws between its hind legs. It barked again; and the bark ricocheted to them through the cold dusk air. The dog licked its lips and its red tongue flashed in the chiaroscuro of the declining light.

Jake whistled to the dog. 'C'm here, c'm here.'

The dog rose, its tail wagging; though it seemed reluctant to approach. Jake pushed on his skis and glided nearer to the dog, whistling, calling it. The dog barked again.

Jake stopped and stepped out of his bindings. He took two steps towards the dog and then he stopped dead. 'Oh my God,' he said.

'What is it?' Zoe came up behind him. The dog was still wagging its tail, looking happy. 'Come on, boy,' Zoe called.

'It isn't a boy,' he said. 'It's a bitch. It's my dog. It's Sadie.'

Sadie was the dog that Jake had grown up with. He'd had her from a pup and she had died when he was eighteen, some years before he'd met Zoe.

The dog, as if triggered by the name, flung herself across at Jake, yelping and wagging her tail. Almost delirious in her happiness at finding Jake, as she jumped up at him she left yellow spots of piss in the snow. Jake fell to his knees hugging the dog, letting her lick his face.

'What's going on?' Zoe asked.

'It's my dog it's my dog it's my dog!' Jake was laughing and crying simultaneously. 'I haven't seen her in years and years, and I missed her, and she's back.' With his knees deep in the snow and the dog licking the tears from his face, he looked up at Zoe, smiling. 'She's back.'

Zoe squatted down by the dog and her husband. 'Jake ... are you sure it's your dog?'

'Sadie, meet Zoe. Zoe, meet Sadie. I can't believe this day! I can't!'

The dog licked Zoe's face, and then went back to Jake. Zoe wanted to share in the happiness, but she didn't believe it. Though she was thrilled to see this new sign of life, she was not a dog lover and had no experience of canines.

'Jake, how can you be certain it's your dog?'

Jake laughed. 'Can you hear that, Sadie? Can you hear that? Darling, if you have a dog, you know it when you see it again. You know it.'

'Okay. It just ... looks like a lot of dogs to me.'

'Listen to her, Sadie! She says you look like any ol' dog! Sweetheart, if I didn't see you in years and years I'd still know you. It's the same thing.'

'Okay. I just … you're not fooling yourself because you want her to be Sadie, right?'

'Here! Without looking, I know she has a scar in the inside fold of her left ear. She got a nasty cut from some barbed wire one time. Come over here.' He held the dog still and pulled back her ear. Zoe peered hard at the pink fleshy exposed part of the inside of the ear. It was true there was a little scar there. Or perhaps it was a shadow. Maybe it was a scar, she thought.

'Phew!'

'This is so wonderful,' Jake said. He got up out of the snow and hugged his wife. 'Come on, let's take her back to the hotel.'

With the dog trotting happily at Jake's heels, they all made their way back to the hotel.

'Do you think the management allow dogs?' Zoe said.

Now they didn't even bother leaving their equipment in the ski lockers; they just left everything in the carpeted lobby, along with their skis boots, gauntlets and coats. Jake went through to the kitchen to find something for the dog. He glanced at the steak still gleaming fresh on the block with the chopped vegetables; then he decided against.

'No old steak for you, Sadie!'

Instead he walked into the freezer and took a steak from the rack. He defrosted it in the microwave and fried it in a skillet. He let it cool before putting it on a plate and offering it to the dog. Sadie wagged her tail and licked her lips, but she turned her nose up at the steak.

'No good, girl? What they been feeding you on here?'

He wondered why Sadie wasn't eating. Any dog would devour a piece of steak regardless of its state of hunger. Jake hunkered down and grabbed Sadie's head just behind each flappy pouch of an ear. He wanted to smell her breath to see what she'd been eating. Thinking he was playing, Sadie licked him. He got a blast of her breath but it smelled of nothing. He tried to remember the smell of a dog's breath.

Fishy, he thought, even when she hadn't been eating fish; and mealy, like biscuit; and earthy like the soil after rain; and like yellow meadow grass; and pond-water; and … *stop*. He told himself to stop. He told himself to stop because this process of remembering made him bring to mind all the things he would never scent or savour ever again in his life other than in memory; and even though memory could restore them momentarily, that thought was bitter-sweet.

He grabbed the dog again, and she licked him, and this time he scented on her warm breath all the things he had just remembered. He walked out of the kitchen and the dog followed him.

He found Zoe in their hotel room.

'Can we have Sadie in the room with us?'

'I'd welcome Sadie's fleas if she had some right now. It's just great to see another living thing.'

'Well, I guess she's another dead thing, actually. I mean, I buried her, in the back garden, years ago. Buried her under a plum tree that had never fruited. Next season and ever after there was tons of fruit on that tree.'

'Nutrients.'

'Or a way of coming back to say hello? Shall I tell you something? I didn't cry when my dad died, but I blubbed like a baby when I buried Sadie. Does that make me a bad person?'

'A bad person?'

'I felt more for my dog. Some people would say there's something wrong there.'

'You didn't care much for what "some people" said when you were alive. Why would you now you're dead? Heck, it doesn't feel right saying that, but you know what I mean. Your father never showed affection. That's what you told me.'

He went to the window and looked out at the darkness creeping over the unimpeachable white that lay on the ground like marzipan on a wedding cake. 'Cold as the snow. Food on the table, clothes on your back, a serviceable education and never a hug. Never once.'

'A different generation, Jake.'

'Well, they got that wrong. If I had a kid I'd—'

'You'd what?'

He turned back to the dog. 'Come here, girl!'

Zoe almost framed a word. But couldn't.

That evening, before preparing for bed, Jake set a blanket down for Sadie so that she could make her den against the wall. Sadie threw herself on the blanket as if she'd always slept there. She lay with her head between her front paws, looking up at them with button eyes. Jake went into the bathroom to brush his teeth. As Zoe pulled back the duvet cover, something happened.

The lights dimmed for a moment, flickered and went out. After a couple of seconds of darkness, they blinked back on again.

Jake came out of the bathroom, holding his toothbrush. 'What was that?'

'The lights went out.'

'I know that. What I mean is why?'

Zoe just stared at him.

'Did they go out all over the resort?'

'No idea.'

'Do you think it was just our room? Or just our hotel?'

She shook her head.

'I wonder what it means,' he said.

Sadie was up on all fours, gazing at him. She barked, once.

'Does it have to mean anything?' Zoe asked.

Jake went to the window. 'The lights are still on out there.'

'Come to bed.'

'I wonder what happened.'

'Come to bed.'

7

In the morning Zoe got out of bed, slipped on her towelling robe and went off in search of breakfast. She wanted to make things as normal as possible for Jake, and a tray of toast, bacon, coffee and juice with a flower filched from the lobby might just do the trick. And that was something: the fresh flowers in their crystal vases seemed in no more danger of wilting than the food in the kitchen. She padded down the carpeted hall and summoned the lift.

The lift door opened and when she pressed the button for the ground floor the chime echoed around her. She'd thought hard about how to make things normal. It was the only way to hang on to sanity. She wanted to hit the ski slopes again. Jake seemed more concerned than she was about the terms of their existence. He'd wondered out loud if they were scheduled to be in this place for eternity. If they were, he'd said, there might be a few more things they would like to do besides skiing.

Zoe had agreed to that. She was just wondering what those 'few more things' might be exactly, in a ski resort, when the lift arrived at the lobby and the doors opened. Zoe gasped, and her hand flew to her mouth.

The lobby was filled with people. They were noisy, animated, chattering and they thronged the reception area. They were mostly dressed in ski gear, but there were others, too, waiting in line at the reception desk, shuffling forwards with suitcases.

Zoe stepped into the throng, still with her hand pressed to her mouth. Behind the desk, three receptionists in smart hotel uniforms were dealing with the new arrivals, looking slightly harassed. One young receptionist, her hair scraped back into a ponytail, pressed a telephone receiver to one ear and held the palm of her free hand against the other. An older woman with copper hair and black-framed spectacles was meanwhile processing a credit card from one of the new arrivals waiting in line. A third was straining to hear what her manager, a thin man in a grey suit, was trying to tell her above the din and commotion in the lobby. Everyone seemed to be talking at once.

Outside the plate-glass doors of the hotel a modern bus arrived. Zoe heard the sneeze of its air brakes as it halted abruptly and parked up. The door opened and the bus began to decant more new arrivals into the hotel.

Elsewhere the concierge Zoe recognised from the day of their arrival was busy with a customer. He leaned on a lectern-like desk of blond wood set aside from the reception, scribbling rapidly on a sheet of yellow paper. His maroon and grey hotel livery shone softly and his bald head reflected the bright overhead lights. A bloom of sweat had appeared on his brow.

Zoe was distracted from the concierge when a man walked past her and gave her a lascivious wink. She caught a whiff of the man's cologne and remembered that she was in the middle of all these people wearing only her towelling robe. She clutched at the robe and tightened the belt. People around her chattered in spirited French, but two women in ski gear nearer to the busy reception spoke in English. She overheard the word 'avalanche'.

She stepped towards the English women.

'Excuse me,' Zoe said, interrupting them, 'did I hear you say there has been another avalanche?'

The first woman turned to her. Her face was flushed, as if she herself had just returned from the mountain slopes. She had the smile-lines of middle age around her eyes. She nodded vigorously. 'Yes, first thing this morning.'

'But is this another avalanche? A fresh one?'

The woman didn't get the opportunity to reply because the young receptionist with the ponytail and the scraped-back hair called both women over to her. Zoe was left waiting, hugging her robe to herself.

The people crowding the lobby didn't seem frightened in any way. Rather they appeared to be excited. Zoe turned to see the new holidaymakers stepping off the bus outside. As she gazed across the lobby, the bald-headed concierge looked up from his papers and instantly spotted her. He raised his eyebrows at her, quizzically.

But Zoe's next thought was: *I have to tell Jake! I have to tell him!*

She skipped back to the lift. It was waiting, open. She hopped inside, flapped at the button and rode it up to her floor. She was giggling. When the lift chime announced her arrival she tried to push open the doors in her haste to get out. She ran down the corridor and hammered hard on the door. 'Jake! Jake!'

There was a grunt and after a few moments he came to the door. He was naked. He yawned like a bear.

Sadie was behind him wagging her tail, wanting to slip past him. 'Where's the fire?'

'Get dressed. Come quick. Leave Sadie there. No, just put a robe on! Quick. You won't believe this! You won't believe it, Jake!'

She was laughing so hard now she was almost convulsing. Jake slipped on his white robe and followed her down the corridor. She grabbed his hand. He wanted to know what the hell was happening.

'Wait and see! Wait and see!'

They got into the lift and pressed the button to go down. Jake blinked at her. She grabbed his face and kissed him hard, slipping her tongue in his mouth. She wanted to stop all his talking and show him the miracle that had happened. The lift arrived in the lobby and the doors opened. Zoe pushed Jake forwards into the lobby and stepped out behind him.

There was only silence.

Nothing and no one. Just as before.

Zoe stopped in her tracks. She stammered something incomprehensible, shaking her head. Then she leapt towards the reception desk, casting around. She looked hard through the plate-glass doors and beyond where the bus full of newcomers had parked. She looked at the concierge's desk. She checked behind the reception desk, where the three women had been working. Then she turned and raced pell-mell outside, through the glass doors and out into the snow.

All was quiet. Everywhere was deserted. There was only the white, white snow of the silent land.

Jake came out after her.

She looked up and down the road. She looked for

wheel tracks that the bus might have left behind. There were none.

'Can't be. Can't be.'

'What happened?' Jake asked.

She ignored him, shouldering him aside to re-enter the hotel.

Back in the lobby, she looked all around for some practical proof that things might have changed; for any tiny forensic scrap of evidence that all those people had really been there, in the flesh and not just in her imagination. She fingered the corners of the concierge's blond-wood desk.

'Come on,' Jake said. He was waiting patiently for an explanation.

'There were people, Jake. Dozens of them. Chattering away. New people coming in with their suitcases—'

'When?'

'Just now! Minutes ago. That's what I rushed up to tell you. Some were talking about an avalanche. One man leered at me.'

'Was it a nightmare?'

'No, he just winked at me. I think my robe was hanging open. I hadn't expected people. They were ... ordinary. It was just ordinary. It's changeover day. People are leaving, people are coming.'

'Do you want a hug?'

'No, I bloody well do *not* want a hug. I'm not mad. They were here. It was busy, but normal. Everything for a moment was back to normal. Like back before ... before it happened.'

Jake blinked at her.

'You don't believe me, do you?'

'Zoe, do you think there is *anything* I can't believe at the moment? But let's think.'

'Hell, I'm thinking, I'm thinking.'

'Right. Can I give you some possibilities without you screaming at me?'

'No. Keep them to yourself.'

'Right. One possibility is that it was a kind of wish-fulfilment. You want everything to be back to normal and for a moment that's how you saw it. Two, it might have been a dream-lag. I've had dream-lags where you get out of bed and the dream won't quite wash out of your brain for a while.'

'Dream-lag? What is a dream-lag? You just made that fucker up!'

'Sort of.'

'Oh, I don't know, I don't know!'

'Come on. Let's get dressed and get out of here.'

As they put on their ski clothes, Zoe described the scene she had witnessed in minute detail. It couldn't have been a dream, she asserted, because there was nothing remotely illogical, uncanny or other than prosaic about it; whereas all her dreams were stamped by the irrational. She went over it again for him, delineating each of the characters she'd seen in the lobby.

Eventually Jake told her, firmly, to put the matter behind her. When they went back down to the lobby Zoe was unable to contain the hope that when the lift door opened again all the people would reappear.

They didn't.

Once outside, Zoe tried to shake off the morning's experience. With Sadie trotting happily beside them, they decided to fully explore the village.

The question of what to do with their time was a pressing one. It seemed to both of them that they had landed the ultimate dream of affluence, one that they weren't sure they wanted. The restaurants and supermarkets were stocked to capacity with food and drink. They could freely take anything, of any quality, from the stores. It didn't even amount to stealing, since nothing in the stores actually belonged to anyone. What's more, they didn't even have to work to maintain this dizzy standard of affluence. Death had delivered to them an idle abundance.

Jake suggested they go shopping. He was simply trying to find a way to comfort her. Shopping normally brought an expression to his face like that of a Nazi at a Jewish Gay Pride festival. But it was his idea.

They went into the ski stores and picked out new ski suits and gloves and goggles. They took new, top-of-the-range ski boots from the racks. They tried them on. The boots were beautiful. But they both found that their old boots were more comfortable, so they left the dazzling new boots in the store for another time when they might need them.

Then they went into the chic boutiques, helping each other choose complete new sets of clothes. Where before Jake would have stood aside with his arms folded, now he joined in with enthusiasm. Zoe laughed at the prices. Jake mocked the displays.

'Where do we stand on fur now we're dead?' he wanted to know.

The boutiques carried every designer label. Zoe had no great interest in clothes but even she could name Prada, Gucci, Vuitton and Fendi, even if only to rail abuse at the fashion victims who made the names famous.

'But look at some of this stuff,' she said. 'It's couture.'

'I ain't heard o' that one,' Jake said.

'It's not a brand. It's handmade stuff, even more expensive than those designer brands.'

'Well. We'll help ourselves to a brace of that, shall we?'

It was fun, for a few minutes, to pick out new trousers and handbags and scarves and shoes. Then Zoe tossed a coat on the floor. 'You know what? I don't want any of this shit.'

'Me neither.'

'Who would be impressed by it, anyway?'

'Not me.'

'And what's the point of taking it back to the hotel? It's here if we want it. Which I don't.'

'Right.'

'Shit, Jake, there must be more to death than shopping.'

'You know I'm on board with that. What else can we do?'

They considered the leisure opportunities, in addition to skiing, afforded by the village. There was of course no TV and no Internet; but they shed no tears for the absence of either. Jake said that watching TV had for the most part made him feel dead anyway, and that the Internet was a murky half-life of random surfing, needless messages, moronic football chat and porn.

'You indulged in football chat?'

'Once or twice,' Jake admitted.

There were spa complexes in several of the hotels, offering saunas and steam rooms. There were sledges by the dozen and Skidoos, if you could get them unlocked, or you could swap your downhill skis for cross-country skis or snowboards. There was ice skating. There were polished granite stones and brooms for some incomprehensible winter sport called Curling. Beyond these opportunities, the entertainment prospects in the village were thin. There was no cinema, but they did find a bowling alley.

So they went bowling.

The machinery was working fine. They even honoured the request to wear proper bowling shoes though they had to discourage Sadie from chasing the bowling balls down the polished lanes. Since neither of them had ever been bowling before, neither knew how to score, so they simply bowled without scoring. It was encouraging to see and hear the balls returned by the operating mechanism with a pleasing click. And the pins made a delightful clatter as they went down. But the pleasure offered by the activity was somewhat limited.

'I dunno,' Jake said. 'I just don't see myself doing this for the rest of my death.'

'I disagree,' Zoe said, flinging a ball down the lane only to see it drop into the gutter. 'I could see myself doing this for at least another ten minutes.'

Pretty soon they had their skis on again and were ascending the mountain by chairlift. Sadie sat between them, panting slightly, tongue hanging out. They planned to take her to La Chamade as a midpoint on the mountain where she could choose to stay indoors or be outside.

'Same logs, still burning,' Jake said after he'd been inside the mountain restaurant.

'That's crazy.'

'It is. I thought I detected a slight shift in the position of the logs.'

'A slight shift?'

Jake had left Sadie in the gabled porch of the restaurant. The dog had wagged her tail as he crunched through the snow back to his skis to rejoin Zoe. 'I think one of the logs was at a different angle. Different from how we left it, I mean. It was leaning at maybe thirty-seven degrees against the other burning log, as opposed to forty-five degrees.'

'Are you serious?'

'I think I am.'

Although she'd initially thought he was joking, she was serious just the same. They both read the details of the landscape avidly; they watched the weather, alert for signs; they studied the condition of the snow, to find meaning or portent; they hunted for cracks in ice and assessed the flow of streams; they scanned the surface of this world for the tiniest signals of change.

And they scanned each other's faces for the same.

'What's up?'

'That shopping this morning,' said Zoe, 'and that bowling. I'm sort of cross with myself.'

'Time wasted?'

'You know me so well. Now that we're ... well, I'll say it, now that we're dead, I'm thinking about my life all the time. What I did. And I'm not thinking about the good or bad things I did. I'm thinking of all the stupid time-wasting things. Shopping. Bowling. Not that I ever went bowling, but the equivalent. Pastimes. Piss-times more like. And it's making me think, is that what this is – all this hammering up and down the mountain slopes on sticks?'

'No, this is different.'

'Why is it?'

He didn't even have to think about an answer. 'Because it's living on the gradient, where you have to stay focused, and you can't switch off or go to sleep for a second; but at the same time as you are the sum of all those lumbering forces trying to stay in control, you are nothing on the enormous mountain, a fleck, a speck of dust, a melting flake.'

'Stone me. You're sounding religious.'

'You don't have to be on your knees to pray. This is me praying. This is me giving thanks, on the knee of the mountain. I'm a moving prayer. See the tracks behind me? Can you read what I wrote there?'

She looked back up the slope and wrinkled her nose. 'It's just tracks. I can't read anything.'

'Yes you can. That's my writing. It's a poem of praise.'

She blinked at him, impressed. He was smiling back at her, a thousand-watt smile. But she said, 'You're fucked up.'

'Maybe. Are you coming skiing?'

He slipped away down the slope and she followed, trying to catch him. His words stayed with her. It was true: they were writing notes of praise on the page of the mountain, she told herself. That's what they were doing.

They raced down the Black-graded slope, skis chattering where the trees had shaded the piste and ice had crusted on the surface of the snow; and the skis whispered and soothed where they emerged into the sunshine and the crust had melted or softened.

After several more runs they checked back at La Chamade for Sadie. She was still waiting in the outside porch. She stood up, tail thrashing as they approached, and followed them inside.

They peeled off their ski jackets and Jake fetched a bottle of wine from behind the bar. He pulled out the cork and was about to pour two glasses when Zoe said, 'Do you hear that?'

He set the full bottle next to the empty glasses on the table and listened hard. There was a distant droning, like engines far-off; or like the movement of heavy, armoured trucks in the distance; or maybe one very large truck.

'Is it a piste-basher?'

They listened again, and the drone became a rumble, sounding indeed like an approaching piste-grooming tractor, but without the beeping electronic alarm. The deep rumbling had an eerie low frequency, muffled and unsettling. It was as if someone had stuffed cotton wool in their ears.

'That's no piste-basher,' Jake said. 'That's the sound of snow moving.'

The low rumbling got louder and brought with it another layer of sound, like a hissing, and when that came the entire restaurant quivered. The bottle and the glasses that Jake had placed on the table began to clink together and work their way to the edge of the table.

The restaurant was shaking. Jake and Zoe were both already on their feet, peering through the window up the mountain. There was nothing to see, but everything to hear. Bottles, crated or racked behind the bar, shivered and clinked. The wine bottle and glasses fell from the table to the wooden floor without breaking. One of the glasses went rolling.

Jake shouted that they should lie down in front of the bar, which lay between them and the source of the sound. He dragged a large table across the floor and jammed it against the bar. They scrambled underneath the table.

'Sadie! Here, girl! Come here!'

The dog was trembling. The rumble had evolved into a cushioned booming, like sustained thunder, and the hissing sound was like that of a huge commercial aeroplane taking off right outside the door.

Bottles tumbled and smashed behind the bar. Plates and other equipment crashed and fell in the kitchen. They heard the wood of the log-built walls actually begin to groan and split. The restaurant threatened to shake itself into matchwood. Zoe and Jake crouched under the table, holding on to each other as the roaring and the sound of splitting wood engulfed them.

At last the shaking subsided, and with it the great hissing and the deep, low roar began to diminish, and pass on over them. They stayed under the table wrapped in each other's arms, both holding the dog.

In less than a minute the sound of the avalanche had dropped to a low thrumming, and then was gone. But the sounds that followed were less easy to identify. There came on the log wall of the restaurant three clear, dull thumps, and then a skittering sound, perhaps like a bird scrambling for bread on the roof. Then silence.

'What just happened?'

'Don't know. Let's wait here a little while longer.'

They stayed under the table until they felt ready to explore. Jake scrambled out, looking uneasily at the roof. Then he stepped over to the wall that had resisted the main burden of snow. The plaster and lath had been smashed in and the snow had forced a gap between the outer logs, reaching long white fingers between them, probing the interior of the restaurant. It was as if the snow had made a grab for them.

'Look at that!'

They couldn't get out of the door through which they'd come in. A wall of snow blocked their way. They left by the kitchen door at the back and skirted the restaurant to see the mounds of snow piled high against the wall.

Zoe was about to remark that that was the second avalanche they'd survived, when she remembered they hadn't survived the first one. Instead she said, 'Can you die twice?'

He turned and looked at her, and snorted.

'Do you think it's like the layers on an onion? That if that avalanche had claimed us, we'd still be here? Or would we be somewhere else? Once I had a dream and in the dream I went to bed and fell asleep and was dreaming. And I knew it. I knew I was dreaming inside a dream. Do you think it's like that? Do you?'

'Are you okay?' he asked, squinting at her.

'I'm fine.'

'You're chattering, that's all.'

'I'm okay. That thing that happened where I thought all the people had come back. It upset me, Jake.'

'Shall we get the hell out of here?' Jake said. 'I'm kind of done with dying today.'

'Done with dying?'

'Skiing. I said I'm done with skiing.'

'No, you said "done with dying".'

'No I didn't.'

'Yes you did. You may have meant skiing but you said dying.'

'Zoe, you've just escaped an avalanche and you're talking gibberish.'

'No I'm not. I'm clear as a bell. I know what I'm saying and I know exactly what you said.'

'Can we please go?'

'Sure we can. Let's get Sadie.'

They went back inside, but they couldn't find her. She was nowhere. They searched the place, calling her name. They knew she was safe because she had been with them under the table. She hadn't emerged from that spot until they did. But now she couldn't be found.

'She must have gone outside.'

They hunted for Sadie in front of and behind the now semi-derelict restaurant building, calling her name across the lengthening shadows of the trees, into the cold. There was no trace, and no paw tracks either. Jake was dismayed by her disappearance, but concluded she must have gone down the mountain.

Zoe made one last search of the restaurant. As she was checking under the tables she heard a burning log spit in the hearth. She turned and looked at the fire. The log that had for so long leaned unmoving against the other had split and fallen, and rolled just a centimetre from its brother.

No more than a centimetre.

8

The loss of Sadie seemed to be a big blow to Jake. He kept speculating aloud about where the hell she could have got to. Zoe was disappointed to lose the dog, too. To distract Jake, she suggested they find a new restaurant to eat in. They'd noticed a beautiful, chic and elegant place called, somewhat ridiculously, La Table de mon Grand-Père.

They chose grandfather's favourite table by the window and lit candles. Zoe took up station in the kitchen and cooked up a boeuf bourguignon that would probably have given the original chef apoplexy; but it was one of Jake's favourites and she served it with buttery mashed potatoes.

Jake waited with his knife and fork upright in his fists, even though he said he wasn't hungry. He wanted to appear enthusiastic for her – she knew it. She kissed his forehead as she placed the plates on the table. 'I've always loved cooking for you,' she said. 'Feeding you. Chopping it all up. Preparing it.'

'You put love into your cooking. I can taste it.'

'Can you still taste it? Here?'

'I would taste its absence, if it wasn't there.'

'You're taking that wine at a clip, aren't you, mister?'

It was true. He'd uncorked a bottle of the most expensive stuff he could find in the place and had already downed two-thirds of the bottle with no help from Zoe.

'I'm trying to get drunk. It's not working.'

'Why do you want to get drunk?'

'The other night, when we drank that champagne and you attacked me in the lift – were you really drunk? Or pretending? Because no matter how much I drink here, I can't get drunk.'

She took a sip of the wine herself. 'I remember thinking I should have been drunk, then I felt drunk. Or maybe I needed to pretend to myself that I was drunk. So can I ask you again why you need to get drunk?'

'Because I don't know what the rules are here! I need to know. I feel like the ground keeps slipping. It scares me, in ways I don't understand.' He poured out the rest of the bottle.

She hadn't yet mentioned to him the burning log in the hearth at La Chamade. 'Something is changing.'

'Yes. I sense it.'

They ate in silence. Zoe wanted to ask if he could taste his boeuf bourguignon, but thought better of it. Instead she asked him if he wanted her to describe being drunk, so that he could feel it; to which he replied he'd like to see if he could make it happen without any help. He got up from the table and came back with another bottle. She decided to join him in the profound loneliness of this hearty drinking.

Outside, a gibbous moon spread waxy light over the deep snow. Jake kept checking to see if there was any sign of Sadie. The pines cast slender shadows at the restaurant, and where the shadows didn't fall the moonlight glittered with unsympathetic beauty on the snow crust.

'I don't think Sadie wandered off. I think she was taken away from us.'

'What?'

'That's what I think.'

Zoe looked at him hard and long. She knew him well enough to know that he didn't mean that some dog-fancier had kidnapped Sadie. She didn't like any alternative idea she could come up with. 'Consider this. Instead of thinking that she was taken away from us, maybe she was given back to you, to us, for that short time.'

He leaned over and twined his fingers in hers. 'You always see the better way. Or choose to.'

'But it's like life, isn't it? We know death is coming. And yet we always see our loved ones as taken away from us, instead of given to us for whatever time they have.'

'You're right. It's just that *right* is hard. It's much easier to collapse and feel sorry for ourselves.'

'I always thought of it as a gift. Life, I mean. I don't know from what force. But I always knew it was a gift. And somehow I think this extra space, this strange extra time right now, has been given to us. For what purpose I can't begin to understand.'

'Admit it. You don't think we're going to be here for ever, do you, Zoe?'

'No.'

She looked into his eyes, and there was something of the moon-on-snow in his gaze as he looked back at her. Earlier when she'd been in the jewellery store and she'd had the prospect of picking out anything – Cartier, Tiffany and the rest – she hadn't wanted any of it. What must it be like to be rich, if you could just pick this stuff up without it creasing your brow for a second? There could be no satisfaction in acquiring anything where there had been no difficulty, no struggle. You would have to have a perverse need to order a dozen or two dozen of the objects in order to feel the pinch. Or only aspire to things that take a bite out of your means. The only jewels she wanted were her husband's eyes regarding her with admiration as he did right at that moment; the only necklace that of his breath on her skin as he kissed her throat; the only ring the simple gold band she already had. She told him all this.

He laughed. 'You're drunk and sentimental.'

'Nope. I'm sober, stone-hearted and clear-eyed.'

'I love you. For longer than this is. Whatever this is.'

'You're the one who's drunk. You only tell me you love me when you're drunk.'

'That's not true.'

'To hell with all that crap about a dessert and a coffee. Shall we walk back?'

They strolled back through the moon-illumined snow, a million diamonds winking on its fragile rime. Jake leaned on Zoe as if he were drunk, though he was not. Before they went inside he held her face in his hands and kissed her in the milky light. She tasted the wine on his kiss; she was sure of it. She didn't have to remember how his kiss tasted; his kisses always tasted of red wine, silk, pepper, the scent of blood, of hope.

Back in the room Jake lurched into the toilet. She heard the sound of his urine streaming in the bowl. Jake always pissed heartily, like a horse. Zoe hung up her ski jacket and closed the wardrobe door behind her. She made to unstrap her salopettes but was interrupted by a familiar musical sound. She turned to mouth something at Jake, who was still busy in the bathroom.

What's that? she had time to say to herself. *It's your … it's your phone, you fool. Someone is ringing you on your mobile phone.*

The cheerful ringtone grew louder.

'Jake!' she shouted.

It's in the wardrobe, Zoe said to herself. *It's in your ski-jacket pocket. You should get it! Go on! Get it!*

But she couldn't. She was paralysed. She heard her own blood rushing in her veins. The sudden intrusion of the ringing phone had her rooted. She made to call out to Jake again. He should be the one to take this call, not her. She tried to move but she felt trapped. Physically constricted, as if something held her arms and legs in a cold grip.

The phone rang again.

'Jake!'

She was back inside the snow tomb of the original avalanche. Packed hard with snow. Upside down, breathing the air from a tiny trapped pocket, trying to move a single finger. She moved a finger, a hand, her arm, and the hard-packed snow around her crumbled, dissolved. She fell towards the wardrobe, flinging open the door to snatch at her jacket. The mobile phone was still trilling. It was in one of her zipped-up pockets. She fumbled with the zip and reached into the pocket. Hands trembling, she flipped open the lid and the square patch of blue light proclaimed *Number Withheld*.

'Number withheld,' she murmured to herself.

She pressed the answer button and lifted the telephone to her ear. There was a voice. A man's voice.

'I'm sorry … I'm sorry, I …' She shook her head in

frustration. 'Slowly please! Je m'excuse, lentement, s'il vous plaît. Plus lentement ... Pardonnez-moi, monsieur ... je ne comprends pas.'

'What's that?' Jake shouted from the bathroom.

'It's a man.'

'What?'

'I can't understand, his accent is so thick ... Monsieur, monsieur, s'il vous plaît, parler plus lentement ... no, no!'

The phone had gone dead. Zoe held the phone at arm's length, stared at it in the palm of her hand, as if it had tried to burn her.

Jake was out of the bathroom, ridiculously holding up his trousers at the waist, wanting to know who she was talking to.

'It was a man.'

'A man?'

'Yes, it was a man.'

'A man? What did he say?'

'I don't know, I just couldn't make it out.'

'But ... Holy Christ!'

'I don't know! I just don't know!'

'Did he ... Was it French? Was he speaking French?'

'Maybe! But I couldn't ... his accent was ... and the line was breaking up. I didn't catch what he said.'

'Can you ring him back? Can you just ring back?'

'He withheld the number.'

'Can you get a line out? Maybe you should try to ring someone again?'

Jake was standing over her now, his fingers trembling just centimetres from her silver phone, as if he wanted to take it away from her. 'But if someone rang in ... I meant back in England. Dial someone at home. Why don't you?'

'Okay. Okay. But Jake – what if he's trying to get through again? The man. What if that man is trying to ring me again? Shouldn't I keep the line free?'

Jake collapsed back on the bed with the palms of his hands pressed flat against the sides of his head. 'Yes … yes, leave it free. He might be trying to get through right at this moment.'

Zoe laid the phone on the table. Then she sank down next to Jake, gripping his arm. Together they waited, staring at the phone on the table, willing it to ring again, terrified that it might.

They watched the phone for twenty minutes. Then Jake sighed and suggested she try to put a call through to England. So she did that; but the results were the same as before. The telephone rang and no one picked up.

'What did the man sound like?' Jake was desperate for tiny details.

'He was hard to understand.'

'But he was French?'

'Possibly.'

'Or Catalan?'

'Might have been Catalan. Or Occitan, for all I know.'

'He spoke French?'

'If it was, he had such a strong accent and the line was so bad I couldn't make any of it out.'

'But how did he sound? What was his demeanour?'

'His demeanour?'

'Yes! His fucking demeanour! Was he agitated? Calm? Urgent?'

'He didn't seem agitated. But he didn't sound calm either.'

Jake took the silver mobile telephone from her hands and examined it, willing it to yield more detail than it could.

They were in no mood for sleeping. They dressed again and went downstairs. Jake quizzed her over and over about the phone call. He'd not heard the phone ringing, only Zoe talking. She asked him how it was possible that he could not have heard the phone. She was almost angry with him that he hadn't heard it. It was important to her. If only he'd heard it, then she couldn't possibly have imagined it.

'Do you think you might have imagined it?'

'That is such a stupid question!'

'No it isn't. Look what happened earlier.'

She ignored the reference to the morning's events. Or non-events. 'I imagined the phone ringing, and then I imagined a voice on the end of it? No, it isn't possible. If you say that again I'll smash you in the face.'

They drank a beer at the bar. Jake served it from the *pression* taps. Wanting to shift the subject away from the mysterious phone call, he started talking about the taste of the beer. He said he would *remember* the taste of it for her, but when he said *hops* and *barley* she said that meant nothing to her. So he said: *Acorns, malt vinegar, sugar, autumn leaves, copper pennies, grief, weak sunlight, laughter, the crust on a loaf of bread ...* until she said, *Stop, I've got it.*

'There's so much in everything,' she said. 'When you take a moment to remember it.'

'Remembering all of this life, or this life that was: it's

like trying to unpack an infinite box.'

'Can you have an infinite box?'

'Look,' he said, 'there's only you and me here to say whether you can have an infinite box or not. There's no one else to say we're wrong.'

'Now I think about everything like that. Every detail, every word, seems intense and packed with significance. I think I was asleep most of my life. If there is a hell, that's the thing I'll be punished for most.'

'Come here. You're on edge. You need to relax.'

They finished their beers and decided to take a sauna. They went down to the spa, where low lights illuminated the swimming pool. They undressed and had a swim while the sauna was heating. Jake had asked so many times where all this energy – the energy that warmed and lit the pool, fired the sauna, heated the hotel – was coming from; so many times that he didn't like to ask the question again. But some part of him knew that it couldn't arrive from a vacuum. With Nature there was always an account; and he said that ultimately they still inhabited a corner of that same infinite box that was Nature.

They made a few lengths of the pool and spent a few minutes floating before going into the sauna. After half an hour in the sauna they found a way out of the spa onto the moonlit snow.

'I've always wanted to do this,' Zoe said. 'Naked in the snow.'

'I still can't feel the cold.'

'It's the effects of the sauna.'

'No,' Jake said firmly. 'It's the effects of being dead.'

'Want me to flog you with birch twigs? You'd feel that.'

Under the flooding light of the moon, Jake did appear to her as a wraith, pale but shining with an inner life. His skin was white like a porcelain carving, but there was a radiance glowing under his skin, and a sheen in his eye that made him seem quick and alive compared to her.

He caught her staring. He smiled. 'Do you think we can fly?' he said.

'What?'

'Since we're dead. Can we jump off the mountain and fly, if we think hard enough about it?'

'I'm absolutely certain we can't. So don't try it.'

'I think it might be possible here.'

She suddenly felt flushed with cold. The effects of the sauna were fading. She pulled a towel around her and stood up. 'Promise me you won't even try such a thing!'

'I was just speculating—'

'Promise me! Promise me you won't dare risk something like that.'

'Okay. I promise. Okay.'

She walked back into the spa. 'Come on. I'm ready to go to bed.'

They left the spa and rode the lift back up to their room. The telephone call had not been mentioned again, but the incident had barely strayed from the forefront of either of their minds. Zoe laid the phone on the bedside table, plugged in, charging, still expecting it to ring again at any time.

Still wanting it to ring again.

It didn't ring, but Zoe didn't need it to keep her awake. With Jake snoring lightly beside her, she lay looking through the window at the ghostly winter landscape. They had taken to sleeping with the curtains open. Old habits were falling away. There was no need for privacy and the light now had become a property of value, a thing that traded in the currency of life rather than death. It seemed an affront to want to keep it out, so the curtains stayed open.

With no snow falling for a couple of days the snow on the ground had become shaped, wind-sculpted now, like a beast that had relaxed its great wings and shoulders and hunkered down. Its smooth edges took a curve, like the roll on white candle wax, and the moon above the trees seemed to make everything brittle, as if at any moment the entire landscape might craze like the paintings of an Old Master.

She had a sudden and dear wish that she could populate that landscape. She felt her belly, trying to detect the smallest sense of bloating or just a little swelling. She placed her fingers on her belly and looked at the moon in the dark sky. Perhaps she was going to have to say something to Jake.

She had lifted a number of tester kits, using them to check herself every day, and every day confirmed the same thing. Positive positive positive. She'd hidden the supply of tester kits at the foot of the wardrobe. She would tell him, she decided again, when the time was right. If they were still in this strange place in a few months' time, her condition would announce itself. With the moon shining brilliantly outside, she fell asleep.

But then she woke and something made her sit up in bed. She felt she had only been asleep for a few minutes but the moon had radically shifted position in the sky, as if working on a different timescale from hers. Some movement, some change of pressure had woken her.

She looked outside and then looked back at the door to their room. The door was open.

Framed in the doorway was a tall man.

There was a moment when her own terror flashed at her and cut her inside like a cold, sharp blade. She made to scream but only a choking sound came out of her mouth. She kicked at her sleeping husband and the physical release made her scream come loud and clear; but now she was up off the bed and ready to fight the apparition in the doorway.

'What? What? What?' Jake was holding her shoulders.

'There was a man! In the doorway.'

For sure the man had gone now, but the door was still open. Jake knew his wife well enough to trust her first report. He sprang to the door and looked up and down the corridor. There was no one, and no sound. He listened hard for doors closing, for footsteps, for elevators. The hotel was silent as the grave.

'Are you all right?'

'Yes. I just woke up and saw him.'

'Did he attack you?'

'No, he was at the door. He didn't come in.'

'What was he doing?'

'He was reaching an arm into the room. Slowly. That's all.'

'What did he look like?'

'He wore black. All-black ski gear. His face was in shadow. I don't know.'

'Heck. Well, he's not there now, darlin'. I swear to you he's not there now. Okay?'

She nodded.

He put his big hands either side of her face. 'I think you could have dreamed it.'

She shook her head, no.

'I think you could easily have dreamed it. We're in a strange place in our heads right now. You could have dreamed it and woken and thought you saw him at that moment.'

'No.'

'You know that place, that moment between dreaming and waking? That's it. That's where we see these things. That's exactly where these things live. You know it.'

'The door was open, Jake! It's still open.'

It was the hole in his reasoning, the gaping puncture. He looked over his shoulder at the open door. 'Did we close it? Did we close the door before we went to sleep?'

'Of course we did.' She marched over to the door. 'Look! Look here!'

On the carpet just outside the door were a few small chunks of dirty snow-ice, just beginning to ooze from crystal to water. 'It's not possible that was from our boots.' Her voice was keening. 'Any snow from our boots would have melted hours ago. There was a man here. That snow says there was a man here.'

Jake turned her around and pressed her back into the room. He closed the door behind him, and dropped the lock and secured the chain on the door for the first time since before the avalanche.

'There are other people here,' Zoe said.

'You don't know that.'

'Yes I do. Other people are here.'

9

They hesitated in the doorway of the hotel, equipped for going out onto the mountain slopes, but afraid. The world – the shadow world, the world of death, of dying, had changed again. The implication that the crisp, white, wide-open, snow-deep slopes were populated reconfigured everything.

Jake barred Zoe's path with an arm across the doorway. 'I think I know what's happened,' he said. 'I think I get it. On the morning of the avalanche, there must have been others. Other people who were killed in the avalanche.'

'And?'

'I think you saw one of them last night. There's no other explanation. The same for the man on the phone. If we weren't the only ones to die at that moment then there would be others, here. Caught here. Just like us.'

'You mean they're coming for us, Jake? I don't want them to come for us.'

'There's no need to be afraid. What if it's just one man, desperately trying to contact us? Imagine how lonely it would be to be here alone.'

'But what would he want? What will *they* want? What will they look like?'

'They'll look like us, of course.'

'You don't know that. Maybe some of them were horribly disfigured in the avalanche.'

'Were we disfigured?'

'No. But I thought about it. What if we can see each other as we were, not as we are?'

Jake shuddered. 'Just don't go there. You've got no reason to think they will look any different from us. Look, the weather is changing.'

He pointed at the clouds in the distance, coiled above the white peaks of the far-off range of mountains to the east. It was an unsubtle attempt at distracting her, but one she accepted gratefully; at least for the moment. Oyster-grey and coral-pink clouds were advancing like an army of aerial wraiths, an army tangled on the impaling snowy horns and bull-necks of the alpine range. But they were supported by reinforcements, fanning out south and north. The pink and grey clouds shimmered with a luminescence both stunning and scaring.

'Red sky in the morning,' Zoe said, and neither wanted to complete a rhyme that completed itself. 'What do we do?'

'We carry on as we have been doing,' Jake said. 'If we encounter someone we just behave as we normally would. But I want you to consider that you may – just may, don't get mad – have hallucinated that man, or even the phone call, just as you hallucinated those people in the lobby. Otherwise you have to be open to the possibility of encountering someone.'

She went to speak but he waved his open palms at her. 'Peace.'

Though Zoe had of course already considered the possibility of hallucination, the notion was of little comfort. Their basic existence in that place seemed like one giant hallucination, so how were they supposed to feel about hallucinatory bubbles inside the hallucinatory bubble? They were still too new to this place to know the currency. If they could remember the savour, the smell, the touch of all earthly sensations, and in the act of memory make them real, then maybe they could manifest other thoughts. This world, this death that was so like a dream and yet so unlike a dream, could be full of possibilities. Perhaps in wanting help to come, Zoe had manifested help. There was no way of knowing if her desire for help was greater than her fear of it.

'Do we go looking for them?'

'I don't want to do that.' Jake said. 'I don't want to go looking for something when I don't even know if it's there.'

'Or if we don't know what it is.'

Jake blinked his bloodshot eyes. They were giving each other lots of space. Their conversations were all the time shrinking in length but expanding in implication. Sometimes Zoe had to ask herself if Jake had actually spoken out loud or had just thought something that she had picked up. Intersubjectivity. Their thoughts were locking together like hexagonal snow crystals.

One of the hotel flags slapped against its tall mast, quite suddenly.

'Bad weather is coming in,' Jake said. 'Let's ski while we can. If there's anyone out there, we'll deal with it.'

The sun was strong and the sky was blue, but a queer blue like a mass of interlocking blue beads, as if it were comprised of pixels. There was an extra chill and a lifting breeze. The thought crossed Jake's mind that later the authorities might close the lifts; then he remembered that there were no authorities other than themselves.

They made their way to the Cadet chairlift to get to the western extreme of the slopes. The Cadet was a modern and speedy apparatus offering a pull-down canopy with a Perspex windshield. They stood side by side in the track and dropped together into the seat. Jake put a protective arm around Zoe as they ascended.

'Okay?'

'Yeah. Think so.'

The fresh breeze on the mountain was scythe-sharp. Zoe shivered, so Jake tugged down the canopy. The windscreen was smeared and crazed; it was difficult to see anything through it, but at least it stopped the wind from biting. Zoe had wanted to scan the slopes. Look for other skiers. But she said nothing.

The chairlift moved forwards in a steady glide, rocking and rumbling slightly at each pylon. The canopy had reduced the sound of the motion to a hiss, though the wind murmured around it like something smoothing its Perspex curves, restlessly searching for a crack or purchase hole for slender fingers.

Jake stared dead ahead through the dirty canopy. He seemed absorbed in his own thoughts. He had less reason to be shaken by the events of the previous evening, she suspected, since he'd neither seen the intruder nor heard the telephone ring out. She understood him well enough to know that he wouldn't write her off as silly or neurotic; but then neither of them knew anything about the true flora and fauna of this place.

If this really were death, or some version of an after-life, then why should it not be populated? Even in the few days that they'd been here she'd made herself adapt very quickly to the idea that they were alone together; and even to try to see that it might be something poetic and wonderful, an elevation of existence rather than a diminishing. It was like a personal Eden, or an anti-Eden. They were an end-of-days couple, not naked in a garden but wrapped in layers in a snow-covered landscape where there were no more apples on the trees and women would no longer have to take the blame, because the old lie had been covered over by snow. But if this were anti-Eden, she had been given strong evidence for the existence of an anti-serpent.

She hoped that the man she had glimpsed in the doorway of their hotel room, and the man on the other end of the telephone, was not the Devil. Zoe shifted in her seat and Jake stirred from his daze. The canopied chairlift rumbled over another pylon.

'Was that our first run down, or our second?' Jake asked at the bottom of the slope.

'This morning? It was our second.'

'I'm losing track.'

She knew what he meant. The snow was so soft and forgiving that it received the skis into itself and it was possible to drop down the mountain in a state of lost consciousness. At one point she looked back up the gradient and calculated that she had skied for three kilometres without any of it registering. It was a pocket of blackness in the white-out. As if she'd gone to sleep. A little death, inside this death.

She didn't discuss this with Jake.

They had become more adventurous, careless even, wandering off-piste through trees, connecting pistes by negotiating silver streams and the jagged, rotten-coloured teeth of rocks. They continued to test the boundaries of their enclosed world, and no matter which point of the compass they followed, they were always, always delivered back to the environs of Saint-Bernard-en-Haut.

It was when they were in the middle of a clump of pine and spruce still heavy with snow, slowly steering a way between the dark trunks, when they stopped at a frozen stream. The ice stream was like a thin, twisted bolt of silk, mysterious and beautiful in the fairy-tale darkness under the snow-laden boughs of the trees. Jake stopped, listening.

'What is it?'

'Shhh. Silence.'

True silence. The freezing of all sound. It wasn't possible, in the modern world, to listen to the sound of true silence. Perhaps not even in the ancient world either: there was wind in the desert; insects in the depths of the forest; wave activity in the middle of the ocean. Nature did not tolerate silence. Only death accepted silence; and there was silence here.

But not even here, Zoe thought. *Because when it gets this silent you can hear your blood in your veins.* There is no silence. And anyway, right at that moment she was hearing another sound. It took a moment to understand what it was. It was the sound of the snow. The massive machinery of something infinitesimal. Billions upon billions of individual snow crystals comprising one blanket of snow were in the process of unlocking.

It was the snow singing to her.

Her heart beat in terror and rapture. She was about to open her mouth to speak when she heard, far off, a dog barking.

'Did you hear that?' Jake said.

'Is it Sadie?'

He nodded. 'It has to be! Which direction?'

They listened again.

Then Zoe heard it again. A single bark. She moved closer to the ice stream and stooped down by the frozen watercourse. 'I know it's crazy but the sound seemed to come from the stream. Is that possible? Can frozen water carry sound? I mean, if Sadie were up the mountain, could the sound of her bark be conducted by the ice? Do you know anything about that?'

'Maybe,' Jake said, his voice full of doubt. 'If a vinyl record or a CD can – why not?'

Zoe listened again to the ice. From there, in the arrested flow and turn and gyre of the stream, came another sound. Human voices, brief, calling.

She stood upright.

'What is it?' Jake said.

'I want to get out of here.'

'But—'

'I have to get out of the trees. Right now.'

She didn't wait for him. She turned her skis down the gradient and slipped between the dark, dry trunks of spruce, made a spinning turn around a rock and dropped through the woods until the growth thinned and she was able to pop out of the trees onto the piste.

There she waited until Jake caught up with her a minute later.

'Sorry. I panicked.'

'It's okay,' he said. 'I've been panicking since day one. I'm still panicking now. I'm just better at hiding it than you are.'

'I heard voices.'

'Human voices?'

She nodded.

'Oh my Christ.'

'They were carried by the ice. No question. No doubt about it.'

'And the dog?'

'The same.'

He pushed his skis between hers and embraced her. 'Come on. If we traverse this slope we can get down to La Chamade. Have a drink of something.'

'Have a drink that doesn't taste of anything.'

'I'll remember it for you.'

La Chamade was almost exactly how they had left it. The wall on the slope side was split and banked with snow. The main entrance was buried so they went in by the rear door. Debris and broken glass littered the floor. Jake kicked a path through with his heavy ski boot and went over to the fire.

It had burned down. It was mostly just soft grey ash, but it was still glowing.

'It's still warm. After all this time, it's still warm.'

He kneeled in front of the embers in the hearth and blew gently. He found some strips of bark to make kindling, laid them over the embers and blew again. Small flames licked at the corners of the bark, and caught. He laid more sticks over the fire and within moments the same fire was alive again.

'Well, that's something,' he said, nodding at his own work.

'What?'

'It means time is running, but at a different speed from … our speed.'

'Time is running.'

They drank, vodka this time because Jake said it didn't taste of anything anyway. He became morose. Zoe thought it was because the bark of the dog had made him sad all over again. He started to throw back the vodka like it was water. She asked him not to, but he said he wasn't drunk, and it seemed to be true, that it had no effect on him.

He shivered, quite suddenly. He looked at her, and the light from outside the window played on his still-bloodshot eyes, and for a moment they looked like watery gems. 'Oh. That's the first time since it happened,' he said, 'that I've felt the cold.'

She wished he hadn't said it. 'Come on. Let's get moving. I think that wind is picking up outside. Maybe that's what you felt.'

'Maybe.'

She pulled on her gauntlets and crunched across some of the broken glass to the rear of the restaurant. But he didn't follow. She turned to see him pouring cognac across the wooden surface of the bar. 'What are you doing?'

'Experiment.'

He opened four more bottles of liquor and doused the entire area behind the bar. She watched with fascination as he stepped over to the fire and plucked out a log that was burning at one end. He tossed the flaming log onto the bar and it immediately ignited the alcohol. The flames made an almost sedate path along the bar until they lit the larger pools of liquor. Within a few moments there was a serious blaze going on behind the bar.

'Let's go.'

They stood off at fifty metres watching the blaze

take hold of the wooden restaurant. Thick black smoke spiralled from the roof.

'Did your experiment prove anything?' she asked, leaning on her ski poles and watching the smoke rise. The wind whipping in from the east was fanning the flames beautifully. Black smoke whorled in the air, dancing over the roof like a djinn liberated from an oil lamp, or from the prison of a perfect white landscape.

'Yes.'

'Are we going to stay here and watch it burn?'

'No need for that. We can go back to the hotel now.'

'Do you think death is making us both a bit crazy?'

'Yes.'

'You go first,' she said. 'I'll follow.'

By the time they got back to the hotel the bad weather coming in had been heralded by the advance force of a strong, scything wind. It flapped at the flags on the poles outside the hotel. It gusted along the streets and herded loose snow into drifts. They had a discussion about whether to go and shut down all the chairlifts they had set in motion. Jake said that was senseless. Zoe said that the wind might damage them, and if that happened they might not be available for them to use.

'It won't matter. I somehow feel that we haven't much longer anyway.'

'Why say that? Why?'

The wind snapped at the flags, threatening to tear them from their proud poles. Jake said nothing and walked indoors. Zoe followed, holding her belly.

She followed him into the kitchen. He walked up to the stainless steel worktop and stood before the chopped meat and vegetables that had remained there since the day of the first avalanche. The pink meat was greying at the edges. It had developed an opalescent sheen. The sliced vegetables were looking a little wilted. Celery had begun to brown where the knife had stripped it so neatly. Peppers had given up the lustre of their outer skins. Carrots were shedding their vivid orange pigment, whitening.

Jake leaned in close to the slices of beef. He sniffed. His nose twitched.

'Let's clear this crap away,' Zoe said.

Jake put out an arm to stop her. 'Leave it all there. It's our only clock.'

But Zoe didn't like what she was hearing. She turned on her heels and went back to their room.

Outside, the wind had turned into a gale. It swooped and moaned and howled around the gables and the eaves of the hotel; mournful, grieving, as if unable to rest in its search for something lost, something that had to be evened out. They watched from the window. A flag had been ripped from the pole and had wrapped itself around a nearby lamp post. An advertising hoarding was blown down flat.

To escape the sounds of the wind they retreated to the spa and turned up the dials on the sauna. They undressed and swam while they waited for the sauna to heat. Zoe thought the water was a degree or two cooler, but chose to say nothing. When the sauna was ready they stepped, dripping, into the pine cabin. Jake ladled water onto the imitation coals.

They sat back, falling into a trance.

'If only we could do something. If only we could act to change our situation,' said Zoe.

'We've been through this. All we can do is exist. For as long as we are allowed.'

Zoe stroked her belly again. The steam rose from the coals. She thought the sauna cabin was getting too hot. 'It's enough,' she said.

'I'm not even sweating,' Jake complained.

'No, but I am.' She took the ladle from his hand and hid it behind her back. 'I have something to tell you.'

'I don't want to hear it.'

'Why not? You have to hear it.'

'Nope. There's a curve in your voice that tells me it's not something I want to hear. In these circumstances, whatever it is, I don't want to hear it.'

'You have to hear it. If you love me, you have to.'

'You think that people who love each other should tell each other everything?'

'Yes, of course.'

'That's ridiculous.'

'Why is that ridiculous, fucker? Whenever I disagree with you it's "ridiculous". Do you know you're just as maddening dead as you were alive? Death hasn't helped you along one bit.'

'You done?'

'Mostly.'

'You want to hear why it's ridiculous? Because two people in love don't make a hive mind. Neither should they want to be a hive mind, to think the same, to know the same. It's about being separate and still loving each other, being distinct from each other. One is the violin string, one is the bow.'

'God help us.'

'Take it in turns, but that's how it should be.'

'Jake: do you have secrets from me?'

'I hope so. And I hope you have some secrets from me.'

'Well, this one can't stay a secret.'

'Come on, then. Let's have it.'

She was about to tell him of the baby growing inside her when the lights flickered and went out. They were left in total darkness in the steam cabin. They waited for a few moments to see if the power would reappear like last time. It didn't. They carefully negotiated their way out of the sauna and across the side of the swimming pool. There was just enough moonlight reflected from the snowy exterior for them to see by.

'Is it the wind?' Zoe said. 'Maybe it brought the power cables down.'

Jake handed her clothes to her without answering.

They made their way back through the darkness of the hotel reception. Jake knew where to put his hands on candles from the restaurant. He made Zoe wait until he returned with a fistful of candles, holding one lighted before him. He led the way back to their room.

Outside the gale had reached a ferocious pitch but the village was well built for storms. They couldn't see any signs of power cables torn down. They left candles burning by the bedside and climbed into bed, holding each other while the wind gulped and sighed and moaned around the eaves. Zoe said she could hear voices in the wind, men's voices shouting. Jake kissed her and hugged her and told her to go to sleep.

Jake could swing wildly from sage to soldier to husband to schoolboy and with breathtaking rapidity. It was one of the reasons why she loved him. They had sex but for some reason he was too gentle with her. After he ejaculated inside her, he laughed; and then immediately burst into tears. He was like a drunk. She held him as his huge sobs subsided, and he drifted off to sleep.

In the middle of the night he woke her. She was groggy, but he was shaking her shoulder. 'Wake up, Zoe – I figured it out.'

She opened her eyes. The lights were on in the room, though the candles were still burning. 'Oh, the power came back.'

Jake looked over his shoulder and up at the lights, as if distracted, or as if he hadn't noticed. 'Oh. Yes. But I worked it out. I know where we are. We're at the place where the laws of physics and the laws of dreaming meet.'

'What?'

'Exactly that. I woke up and realised it.'

She pulled him back to the bed, closer to her. 'Go back to sleep, darling. Back to sleep.'

'Yes.'

He did so instantly. She got out of the bed to switch off the electric lights. An almost full moon had emerged from behind the clouds to shine waxy, brilliant light onto the snow outside. It reminded her of her father. She lay there looking at the moon, as if it had secrets, as if it had knowledge.

10

Her father had said, *You should hold on to every single moment of life, Zoe, because it runs away, runs away so fast.* And he would know: lost both parents before he was out of short trousers, then a brother in a car smash, and then a lovely sister who had slipped on some ice on her way to church and didn't she crack her skull? Then of course Zoe's own mother. *It can be all over like that, Zoe, like that.*

He wiped two forefingers together to show what *like that* was all about.

Zoe had been over at his house doing the tree. She'd done the tree for him every year since her mother had died. They'd had a dispute about it. Not an argument exactly. But Archie had said what was the point when he was going to be away over Christmas? But she'd said it wouldn't be the same without the tree.

Archie was a retired engineer from Dundee, working-class boy made good. He moved into the bungalow on a development for retired persons after selling his own comfortable house and giving the remainder of the pro-ceeds to Zoe and Jake, so that they could buy their own house. The development had a warden and a bell-push to alert the warden if you had a fall or got into dif-ficulty. Archie had immediately disabled the bell-push. Said it was a bloody insult.

Yes, hold on to every moment, Zoe.

But what was a moment? Spindrift on the back of a sunlit wave? A fox's tail as it disappears through the hedgerow? A meteorite as it flares in the August night sky? Everything is ending or becoming. Zoe didn't believe you could freeze a moment, or hold on to one.

Archie had stood watching her decorate the Christmas tree, his fists dug into his hips. He was the sort of bloke who always wore short-sleeved shirts, whatever the weather. It showed off his tanned and hairy arms, but Zoe knew it wasn't vanity that made him wear short sleeves: it was that sleeves just got in the way and needed to be rolled up all the time.

Archie had booked a winter holiday at a hotel in Tunisia with two of his cronies from the Bowling Club. Jake was to pick them up in the morning to taxi them to the airport. He hadn't wanted Zoe to decorate the Christmas tree because there would be no one there to see it, he said.

Zoe said, 'If a tree falls in the woods with no one there to see it, does it still make a sound?'

'You bloody what?'

What Zoe knew was that Archie didn't want the tree because each year he was finding the memories harder to take.

The Christmas tree in their household had been different. Different from other people's trees, that is. Rather than being decorated with coloured baubles it was hung with memorial objects. It had all started when Zoe's older sister was born thirty-four years ago. Her mother and father had started to hang on the tree objects that represented some significant event in their lives. Each birthday, anniversary, family holiday was represented.

If they went away on holiday they bought something to hang on the tree. If the children passed an exam or some other milestone, a symbolic object found its way onto the tree. There were silver Christening gifts, a tiny ballet shoe, a silver box containing all their milk-teeth, a swimming badge, shells and stones brought back from beaches and drilled by Archie, amulets purchased from street vendors in exotic places ... and gradually there had been no room for coloured baubles as the tree became a memory map of their days together and apart. Moments of ending and becoming, hanging on the branches.

It was a Tree of Life, in the real sense. And Archie was finding it harder to look at it each year.

He stood watching her assemble the tree and shifted his hands from his hips to dig them deep into his trouser pockets. 'Aye, we're just snowflakes on a griddle, lovely girl. Snowflakes on a griddle.'

'You don't know what comes after,' Zoe said, draping a bracelet on a branch of Blue Norwegian spruce. 'Nobody does.'

'Nobody wants to know, you mean. Nobody likes to know. It's just a long dark ride with your eyes shut and your ears plugged. Anyway, it's not about where you're going. It's about what you leave behind. Now the Muslim, he—'

'You told me that, Dad.'

Archie continued anyway. He always spoke about 'the Muslim' as if there was only one. 'Now the Muslim, he says you should dig a well for the generations that come after you. I like that. I do.'

Archie had dug his wells. He had built bridges and been responsible for constructing two major dams in countries abroad. No one ever needed to tell Archie to roll up his sleeves.

'No one knows,' Zoe persisted. 'It's the great mystery.'

'Ah, you say that, but.'

Zoe waited for him to go on, though with Archie nothing ever came after the *but*.

Then he said, 'See your mother? She didn't believe in it either. See how people say they're haunted by a ghostie? Well, your mother made me a promise that if there was an afterlife she would *never* come back and haunt me. So if I saw her as a ghostie ever, then I would know it was in my head.'

'And did you see her?

Archie sighed and sat down in his favourite chair. He settled back, spread his legs wide and seemed to stare at a spot on the wall. After a while, he said, 'Everywhere.'

Zoe stopped decorating the tree and settled at Archie's feet, resting her head on his knee. He ran his fingers through her hair, as he would when she was a little girl. 'Everywhere. It took me three years to stop pulling two cups from the cupboard if I wanted to make some tea. She'd be behind me. If I got out of the bath she'd be standing there holding a towel for me. Or I'd be watching the TV and I'd laugh at this or that or I'd want to say would you believe it and I'd look up at her. She was everywhere.'

'Dad.'

'And then it fades and you don't want it to and re-membering gets harder. And sometimes you need help remembering. I love that tree and I don't, but. Come on, up you get, finish the job.'

Archie was a great one for finishing a job.

After she'd done the tree she helped him pack his suitcase, though he was ready. 'Jake will be here for you at seven in the morning. Have you told Bill and Eric?'

'It's good of him. He doesn't have to, you know.'

'He wants to. He likes you.'

'It's good of him. You're both too good to me.'

'I know. You need a shave. Come on, give me a kiss, I've got to get back.'

'Did they get off all right?' Zoe asked Jake when he returned from the airport the next day. 'I thought he was looking tired yesterday.'

'Tired? They were like three teenagers. They've got bowls tournaments and afternoon tea dances lined up. They reckon they're going to pull some old biddies. Don't be surprised if he comes back with a girlfriend.'

'So long as she's over sixteen I won't mind.'

A week later, two days before Christmas, it was Zoe's thirtieth birthday. They had some friends round for a dinner party. They drank a lot and laughed too loud. Then around the time the coffees arrived someone said that thirty was a significant birthday, and everyone around the table agreed. Someone else said it was the first time you heard the bell.

What bell? someone asked.

But they all knew what bell. It was like you'd already completed a few laps, observed another, but this was the first time you'd properly heard the bell. There had been one at seven but you hadn't heard it because you were so young; and then one at fourteen but you hadn't heard it because you were so busy looking over your shoulder; then another at twenty-one but you hadn't heard it because you were too busy talking; and then one at twenty-eight which for some reason took two years before you heard it. But they all agreed you did hear that one, eventually.

Your lousy career, said one guest. Babies, said one of the women. Lovers, friends, travel, said another. Parents ageing. Bong. All the things you hadn't done. Might not do. Bong.

And in the silence that came after the bell someone said, 'Happy Birthday, Zoe, cos you're one of the best.'

'Yes, happy birthday.'

'Happy birthday.'

After the guests had gone home, Zoe and Jake cleared away the debris of the dinner party and went upstairs. Jake crashed out on the bed and fell asleep immediately. Zoe felt dizzy from the wine. She lay down on the bed and her head was swimming so she stretched out a leg and pressed her foot flat on the carpet to try to stop the room from going round and round. Eventually she fell asleep.

She was awoken some hours later by someone shining a bright light in her face. She sat up and blinked into the white light, shielding her eyes with one hand.

'Who's that?'

There was no reply.

She looked over her shoulder at Jake, who, illuminated by the light, slumbered on.

'Who's there?' she tried again.

No one answered.

She swung her legs out of bed and it was then that she realised the light wasn't coming from a torch inside the room. It was streaming through the window. Jake had failed to close the curtains properly before crashing into bed and this light was flooding in from outside. She went to the window.

It was the moon. Thrilling, waxy and low in the sky, it seemed supernaturally large; like an inflated berry of mistletoe, or a pearly bauble hanging on a Christmas tree. She gasped. Its light looked milky, liquid, sticky even. She could easily see the crater shadows on the moon. It was almost like an unblinking eye, gazing in at her from the clear night sky, remote yet interested. Never had she seen it so low in the heavens. It seemed to risk crashing on the earth.

There was some music in the distance, light orchestral music, drifting over the rooftops. She assumed someone else was having a dinner party. The music swelled and then dropped away, as if swirling on a breeze.

She glanced over her shoulder at her sleeping husband and thought about waking him; but she resisted the idea, afraid of killing the moment. So she stood at the window, gripping the hem of the curtain, staring back at the moon, holding her breath.

She was uncertain how long she'd watched the moon, but after a while, without any sign of movement or sense of time passing it seemed to have retreated, and faded; withdrawing to a condition of ordinary beauty.

She went back to her bed and lay down, still watching through the window, and eventually she drifted back to sleep.

In the morning over breakfast, while they were both getting ready for work she started to tell Jake what she'd seen.

'You should have woken me.'

'Yes. Now I'll never know if I dreamed it.'

He was about to answer when the telephone rang. It was Eric, Archie's friend, calling from Tunisia. 'Zoe, my love, I want you to be sitting down.'

When he said that she already knew everything.

'I'm so sorry, my darling. I'm so sorry.'

'When?'

'Bill and I missed him at breakfast, so we went up to his room.'

'I see.'

'I want you to know how happy he was last night. How happy. We'd been to a tea dance in the afternoon. He didn't stop giggling. We danced with all these lovely ladies. Then in the evening we had a lovely dinner and we drank some wine and after that we went for a stroll along the seafront. The moon was incredible last night. Beautiful.'

'I know.'

'Archie was dancing. He was whisking an imaginary partner along the promenade. He wasn't drunk, you know your dad. But he kept saying look at the moon, look at the moon, lads! Are you there, my darling? Are you there?'

'Yes.'

'Look at the moon, he said. I've never seen your dad so happy, my darling. Bill said the same. He was a lovely man, was Archie. A lovely man. I'm so sorry.'

'Couldn't help himself,' Zoe said. 'Had to come visit me despite himself.'

'What's that, darling?'

'Nothing.'

'I had to call you. He was a wonder to us. Are you there, sweetheart?'

Jake, who was watching her face when the tears

started rolling, took the phone from her and held her hand as he continued the conversation with Eric, very softly.

Eric and Bill had insisted on taking care of everything. Archie's insurance was up to date and they dealt with the officials and the paperwork and had Archie flown back in a zinc-lined coffin, as per the regulations. Archie's remains were cremated at the local cemetery. He had a Humanist service.

Zoe left the Christmas tree in his bungalow until Twelfth Night, according to the tradition. Then she carefully packed away all the hanging mementos. She made charity bags of his decent clothes and asked Eric and Bill to take what they wanted of his equipment. She kept a few things for herself and gave them Archie's bowls to pass on to someone at the club.

Eric asked her about something she'd said on the morning he had phoned her from Tunisia. 'You said he had come back to you, despite himself. What did you mean?'

So she told them the story of the moon. Eric and Bill both looked at her with shining eyes, and said nothing.

Zoe took the box of Christmas tree tokens and souvenirs so that she and Jake could continue the tradition of decorating theirs with luminous memories. She went out and bought a silver-moon disc to commemorate Archie's passing and all those years afterwards, whenever her eyes fell upon it as it hung from the tree, it never once made her sad.

11

The wind had died down and the entire resort had a scraped look, as if raked clean by a giant claw. Loose snow had been swept and piled high against doors and apartment blocks; parked cars had been shaved of ice and snow on their windward sides; and the entire village seemed to have been blown back at a minute angle, only now emerging to blink in surprise at the morning sun.

Every cloud had been chased from a sky rendered the thrilling lapis lazuli of a Pharaoh's death mask. The early-morning sun had been reborn white-gold.

'Today is the last day that I intend to ski,' Jake declared.

'Oh?'

'It's stunning. These are perfect ski conditions. We will never get another day like this. I want to finish on this high.'

'Why do you need to finish at all?' There was a slight tremor in Zoe's voice, one which she couldn't hold back. It was as if Jake was declaring a loss of faith in some religion. 'Why not ski while we can?'

'I think our time is limited. I can't tell you why. I just sense it. And I've stopped enjoying it.'

Zoe didn't argue. Jake seemed resigned. But she didn't believe it; couldn't believe it. This was not the end. He had been into the kitchen that morning and had reported that the beef on the stainless steel worktop was beginning to smell. His clock was running. But she, after all, was running an anti-clock in her belly.

She was still testing regularly, and in every case the test was positive. The baby was still alive inside her and she knew, in a way that required no test, that it was thriving. It might be no bigger than a fingernail, a crescent moon in a vast night sky, but she felt it drawing on her, feeding on her every heartbeat. While it was growing, while it was quickening – and she didn't care how old the foetus was because she felt the tapping of a butterfly's wing no doctor would ever convince her was gas or stomach pains – this could not be the end for them.

She wanted to shout this to Jake but didn't have the strength. It just seemed absurd to philosophise about their predicament. She couldn't accept that this 'death' was to be one long debate. She knew that this baby was alive inside her and that it would come to term. She didn't know what would happen at that moment. It was just unimaginable to be in death and pregnant at the same time. Unless Jake were correct, and they were all the twisted offspring of some marriage between physics and dreaming.

Jake had gone out of the hotel to put on his skis. Zoe clumped across the lobby behind him. As she crossed the lobby she dropped one of her ski gauntlets and bent down to pick it up.

As she did so she heard the unmistakable sneeze of the air brakes of a luxury bus, and as she straightened up, glove in hand, she almost dropped it a second time.

There was the bus parked outside the hotel, and the lobby was thronged with chattering people all over again. The babble of their voices filled the air. Zoe could feel the warmth from their bodies as they crowded the lobby space and they all spoke with great animation.

She turned back to face the reception desk and the same three women were in place, in their smart hotel uniforms, each engaged in exactly the same activities as when she had first seen them. The young woman with the ponytail had the phone pressed to her ear. The lady with the auburn hair and black glasses was processing a credit card, and the third receptionist struggled to hear what her grey-suited manager was trying to say above the racket.

The people were mostly dressed in ski gear, apart from the arrivals coming in trailing their suitcases-on-wheels. Though she was standing in a different part of the lobby, the same man came by and winked at her. She caught a whiff of his cologne all over again. She had to check to make sure she wasn't wearing her towelling robe as before, but no, she was properly equipped with ski gear this time. She turned to the reception. There were the two English women talking about an avalanche.

Zoe felt her breath coming short. She looked out through the glass doors to see if there was any sign of Jake. But there were so many people thronging the lobby, and both they and the newly arrived bus obscured her view of the road outside.

Bewildered, she was about to turn to speak to the two English women at the reception desk, but at that moment the concierge at his blond-wood desk happened to look up and catch her eye. He raised his eyebrows quizzically, and then opened his eyes wide, as if suddenly remembering something. 'Madam!' he called to her. 'Madam!' He raised an arm high, fluttering his fingers at Zoe in a come-hither motion.

Zoe was at first mesmerised by the concierge, who was smiling and beckoning. Then she was sure that he was not calling to her, and that he was after all beckoning some other person behind her, perhaps someone at the reception desk. She turned almost a half-circle to look over her shoulder.

But there was no one behind her. No one at all.

The English women, the three receptionists and their manager and the people waiting in line at the desk had all gone. The sound of animated voices had been sucked away. Even the whiff of cologne had vanished from the air.

Zoe turned back and the concierge had disappeared too, along with all of the other skiers and hotel residents, and along with the luxury bus that had parked outside. She could now see, through the plate-glass doors, Jake waiting for her to come out.

She paused for a few seconds, then glanced back again at the empty reception desk before leaving the hotel. Jake was standing with his legs apart and his arms folded. He smiled. It was obvious that he'd seen none of it.

'You okay?'

'I'm fine,' Zoe said.

From the very top of the mountain, and with the great coin of the sun imprinted in the sky behind her, she watched Jake ski. He swooped down the slope ahead of her, executing perfect turns, carving the snow, attacking the slope. His long shadow raced ahead of him like an independent spirit. She'd never seen him ski so well. He seemed to have mastered technical perfection. Though she had always been the superior skier, there was no doubt that now he was outstripping her in ability. She watched him speed through the trees at the bend in the slope, and disappear over the next rise.

She set off after him, determined to catch up. But her early turns were cumbersome, poorly executed. At one point she let the tips of her skis cross and had to pull up to compose herself. She was exasperated that while Jake appeared to have perfected his technique, she seemed to be moving backwards. Perhaps it had been the second hallucination of people thronging in the lobby that had so unsettled her. Or perhaps it was the presence of the baby, unconsciously urging her to caution. A fall could be dangerous. She had good reason not to want to attack the slope.

The awesome silence of the place crept up on her. The spruce and pines, all still loaded with snow, spread their limbs in a frozen ballet, breathing a ghostly incense from dark, arid chapels sheltered by their branches. She inhaled the cold, wine-sharp air deep into her lungs. *Grow, baby, grow. We will cheat death.*

She said this to herself defiantly, but considered it might be an affront to some angry God of the underworld. She looked down the slope. Her shadow stretched ahead of her for maybe twelve metres. Then she noticed a movement, a faint twitch at the periphery of her vision.

Next to her own, there were other shadows.

On her right-hand side was a cluster of shadows, roughly human in form, swaying gently. The dark shapes were clearly imprinted on the snow ahead of her. She stopped breathing. She dared not turn her head to look behind her. There she could feel the presence of several beings. Perhaps they were people. Perhaps not.

She kept her eyes on the swaying shadows, convinced that they were unaware she had spotted them. Her skin prickled. It flushed cold and became an abrasive substance, like sandpaper. She felt the fluid in her eyes freeze.

There were perhaps five or six of them, huddled in a group. It seemed incredible that they hadn't seen her. She could hear them talking, murmuring quietly to each other. She studied the outline of their shadows on the wax-like snow. They were certainly human in shape but with extra tall limbs like long poles or long-stemmed trumpets emerging in front of them, perhaps from their mouths. They were moving, advancing towards her, and yet at the same time not seeming to come closer.

Zoe was already standing with her poles at the ready. She made her limbs unlock, flexed her feet in her boots, preparing to make her fastest descent down a ski slope ever. At the last moment she took her gaze from the moving shadows, and with an insane sense of defiance, she turned her head to meet her adversaries eye to eye.

She almost slipped backwards. There was nothing.

Behind her was the crest of the slope, and beyond that the great, forbidding and crumbling horn of a white mountain peak, goring the blue sky. Beyond that the implacable sun.

The shadows too were gone. There was nothing there, and nothing indeed that could form a shadow. Seconds earlier there had been people – or things – behind her.

She had felt their breathing. She had heard their low murmuring voices. Now, nothing. Only the horn of the mountain nodded back at her, unconcerned.

She waited in a kind of shock. The idea that she had somehow hallucinated the presence of other people – other beings – was untenable. Their moving shadows had been cut clear into the white snow. Their voices had been made buoyant by the chill air. Their breathing had almost tickled the nape of her neck.

Now their absence was almost as terrible as their presence. For the first time she wondered if this place might be inhabited not by other people, not by other ghosts, but by something she might call demons. She needed to catch up with Jake. She flexed her grip on her poles and turned her skis in the snow.

Then her phone rang again.

The sound plucked her out of her terror and triggered her back into another. The playful signature call was coming from the inner pocket of her ski jacket. Her gauntleted hand flew to her jacket and she fumbled with the zip, but the padded fingers of the gauntlet were too thick to pull the zip open. She was afraid she wouldn't get to the phone before the caller hung up.

She dropped her ski pole and tore the gauntlet off her right hand as the signature tune played louder inside her jacket. Her fingers fumbled at the zip and clawed inside her pocket, at last folding around the cold metal curve of the ringing phone. She flipped open the cover and pressed the phone to her ear.

'Hello? Hello? Who is it?'

It was the same voice on the line again. A gruff male voice, speaking in a language or accent she couldn't understand. The line wasn't clear. It was muffled and distant and the man seemed to be repeating the same phrases over and over.

'I can't hear you! Please! Je ne comprends pas!'

The voice barked an instruction or phrase at her.

'Encore! Say again! Oh God! Please! Who are you?'

The voice spoke again. He seemed to say the words *la zone, la zone*. But the line crackled. It was impossible to know what he was saying. He might have been calling from the dark side of the moon.

The line went dead.

La zone. Or was it *La Zoe*? No, no. It was more like *la zone*. He might have been saying that. He might have. *The zone.* But what did that mean?

Zoe turned her skis to the fall-line and let them slice through the fluffy snow. She dropped a few hundred metres in seconds. Jake was waiting for her.

'Skiing good,' he said as she carved a turn to draw up beside him.

She looked at him. His huge sunglasses shielded his eyes, bouncing the sun's glare back off the blue glass. She wondered how much to tell him.

'You okay?'

'The phone went again.'

'What?'

'Same voice. Same incoherent words.'

'You're not okay. You didn't—'

'No, I didn't imagine it. Why does it only ring when you're not there? I'm going to give you my phone. You can handle it next time this happens.'

'No, you keep it. I have my own.'

'I thought he said *la zone*. The zone. But that might be wrong. I don't know. It was so muffled and distant.'

'The zone.'

'Maybe.'

'Come on. Enough. Let's call it a day.'

They had no appetite for food that night. Jake re-inspected the vegetables and the meat on the slab in the kitchen and reported that they were finally going off. The celery sticks were browning. A grey patina was forming over the chopped potatoes. But it was all still happening very slowly.

They went out to a bar. They found a CD of songs by The Kinks and drank rich, dark, juicy Malbec; but they couldn't be bothered to remember how it tasted or how to be drunk. The music they loved gave them little pleasure, as if that too had to be remembered. They ran out of conversation, so they went back to their room early and showered.

Zoe noticed Jake's erection as he dried himself. She made some comment.

'It's odd. I'm hard all the time here.'

'All the time?'

'Yes. Well, it subsides for a little while after we've had sex but not for long.'

'You should say.'

'Sweetheart, I can't be inside you all the time. You know you wouldn't like it.'

She raised her eyebrows at him.

Their sexual activity had regulated a long while ago. She had never used it, like some women, as a means of getting her way on other matters. But she had never made herself open to him either. She had always controlled the flow. Sex was never rationed; but neither was it unrestricted. He liked to have her from behind; she didn't. He liked to do it outside; she wasn't much for that. He liked her to sit astride him; she preferred conventional positions. He occasionally suggested dressing up; she found the idea too bloody ridiculous for words.

'I've been a disappointment to you in that department, haven't I?' she said.

'No you haven't,' he countered.

'I've been lazy.'

'Not true.'

'It doesn't mean I loved you any less.'

'I know that.'

'Sex isn't a measure of love. Sometimes it has nothing to do with love. Nothing whatsoever.'

He sat on the bed in his towel, and put an arm around her shoulders. 'Why are you saying all these things?'

'Because here it feels like I have to make everything I say count for something.'

'Didn't you before?'

'No. Not always, anyway. I was careless with things I said. I was careless with my decisions. Careless.'

'Maybe it doesn't matter any more.'

'Oh, it does matter. Everything matters. And in this place the rules are different.'

'In this place we make up the rules, it seems to me.'

She sighed. She knew her words had depressed him a little. He'd simply come at her wanting a fuck and she'd disheartened him. But if there were to be no lovemaking that night it would represent the first pause since the day of the avalanche. Zoe didn't want to allow that to happen. If a night went by, then the next day might, too; and then the next night. And what Zoe feared most was the wedge.

She couldn't say exactly when she had started to feel

the presence of the wedge. It might have begun in those very first days when they had argued about how to get out of this place. But she felt that some force, some power like magnetism or anti-magnetism was doing its best to quietly insinuate its way between them. Again it was like a law of physics, some current grounded in the place that behaved like another woman who wanted to split them up, through barely perceptible and insidiously manipulative means.

Her pregnancy was intimately connected with this feeling. She was still testing obsessively. And each time confirmation that the baby was swelling inside her was offered, then so did she become attuned to the possibility of a division between her and Jake. This was nothing to do with love or lack of it. Her love and affection for him, and their mutual dependence in this shadow world, had amplified massively. But there were forces of reversal at work here. If love was a force of gravity, this place had a centrifugal force, dragging at her psyche.

She wanted to arm herself against this centrifuge and sex was part of her armoury. She placed the flat of her hand on the rise of his belly and then leaned across him to lick a sensitive spot just above his pelvis, because it would always make him spasm. He kicked. She spat into her fingers and rubbed the saliva under the head of his cock and squeezed him. His cock grew harder in her hand.

She slipped his cock inside her mouth, sliding her tongue around the glans, and as his cock grew even harder and swelled in her mouth she felt his body give in to her and become limp by contrast. He lay back, surrendering to her, giving her all the power. She released his cock and sat upright, swinging her leg over him, to mount him. Outside the alpine light was a mysterious species of blue she associated with neon, almost ultraviolet. It illuminated his teeth and the whites of his bloodshot eyes and gave his limbs a tanned, healthy hue.

He had once said to her that she was such a sexual creature she could make a dead man come, and here she was, proving it. She levered herself onto him, impaling herself, gasping at the moment of yield when her vaginal muscles relaxed and let her slide down over him. She leaned forward, letting her long hair fall across his face, inhaling the smell of his hair and his sweat. The smell of fuck charged the room, circling above them like smoke, like a ghost. She pressed her fingertips against the white wall over the headboard above him to give herself leverage, raising and lowering herself onto him. She was fucking him hard and angrily and with a desperate air, as if this might be their very last time. The headboard was banging against the wall as she thrust with her pelvis, thudding against the wall, and she didn't stop even when she felt him ejaculate and shiver as his orgasm eclipsed him entirely. She went on, driving herself, slamming the headboard against the wall until she started to feel the wall itself crumble under the touch of her fingertips, turn to powder, dissolve until it was no longer the powder of plaster but the powder of snow, freezing to the touch, and collapsing back into a swirling, gaping hole, from which a man's arm reached through and took her by the neck, took her by the throat in an icy grip, closing off her breathing, pulling her, trying to drag her off Jake, choking her until she shrieked out loud, not in ecstasy but in terror.

Jake sat up. 'What is it? What is it?'

The outstretched arm released her, and the pool of snow, the swirling white hole in the wall simply closed up, becoming white painted plaster on a bedroom wall all over again.

Now Jake was holding her face between his two large hands, his eyes searching hers for explanation.

She looked at him; she looked at the wall. 'I'm seeing things. Jake. I'm seeing things.'

'What things?'

'Nightmarish things.'

'Tell me.'

But she shook her head. She'd recognised the arm that had come through the wall. She recognised the ring on the middle finger and a small scar on the back of the hand before it had started to choke her.

They lay together for a while, he stroking her hair. But even with his eyes closed he could almost see her restlessness, and he said so. 'Go to sleep, my darling, go to sleep.'

'No. I can't. I have to talk to you.'

'I never like the sound of that.'

'I feel like this is a chance to pull a thorn out of my skin. It's about Simon.'

'Yes. Best man at our wedding. I know about that.'

She blinked at that. 'Yes. I always feared you knew.'

'Can we leave it?'

'It was a bad time for me. You weren't paying me much attention. I'm not saying it was your fault. I'm telling you it was meaningless, mistaken and a folly. That's all. I knew you knew, all along. I just needed to have it said in the open.'

'Feel better now?'

'A little.'

'Well, don't expect me to feel better. You've taken the thorn out of your skin and stuck it in mine. And it hurts.'

'I'm sorry, Jake. I'm sorry.'

'Don't cry. It doesn't matter. If there is any sense to marriage at all it's so that I take your thorns, and you sometimes take mine.'

They lay together in the dark of the room. There was enough light reflecting off the snow from the lamps outside by which to see. Nothing more was said.

After a while Jake's breathing changed: he had fallen asleep. Zoe fell asleep too, but woke shortly after when she heard the gentle sound of harness bells outside.

They were the kind of bells associated with animals in train, of distractions for tourists. Zoe glanced at Jake's sleeping form and swung her legs out of bed. The harness bells had stopped. She moved over to the window.

Since they had moved across the hall, their window looked down onto the road passing the entrance to the hotel. And there stood the vast shadowy form of a splendidly muscled black shire horse harnessed to a large sledge. It was a stallion, its flanks sleek, coal-black and sparkling with fresh sweat. The breath from its muzzle steamed in the cold air like an old engine at a railway platform. The animal's hooves were magnificently feathered and on its head it sported a brilliant crimson plume that in the moonlight was the colour of spilled blood. The horse chewed at its silver bit, but otherwise remained perfectly still, as if waiting.

Zoe gasped at the sight of the creature. She stepped

back, automatically reaching a hand to wake Jake, but changed her mind. Throwing a blanket around her, she hurried out of the room and took the elevator down to the lobby. She ran out barefoot in the snow, hardly conscious of the cold.

It was still snowing. Large fluffy flakes, some already clustered as they fell. The horse stood utterly immobile as she approached, doing nothing to acknowledge her presence.

It was an enormous stallion, powerful in its withers and boasting a great curve of muscle at its loin quarters. Zoe knew enough about horses to estimate that she was looking at one a staggering twenty hands high. Though the horse wasn't saddled for riding, to mount such a beast would require a small ladder. She put a tiny hand to its flank and felt its hairy and muscular warmth. Snowflakes dissolved the instant they fell upon its steaming sides. Rows of tiny bells were stitched into its polished-leather harness, and the metal foil of each bell was stamped with the emblem of a six-pointed snowflake.

The horse waited patiently, as if for a command. Zoe moved her hand along its shoulders and neck, failing to reach the poll between its ears, so tall was the horse. Though the horse pricked up its ears at her gentle lunge, and clouds of mist spiralled from its muzzle.

'So black against the snow! You are beautiful!' Zoe said. 'Beautiful!'

She moved to the front of the horse. Its nostrils were terrifying, flaring black holes releasing snorts of steam. It was like a creature from the origins of the universe. The horse turned its head slightly away from her, so that its eye, regarding her steadily, was like a polished black obsidian mirror in which she could see herself distorted: a small thing, swathed in a single blanket, looking up with hope and wonder. The horse tossed its head and shook its crimson plume, and began to chew again on its bit. Zoe tried to blow gently into its nostrils but it shook its plume at her again. She took it as a sign that he didn't like her approach from the front.

Instead she walked around the patient animal to examine the sledge it was pulling. It was a simple construction: a heavily built wooden frame with giant steel runners to glide over the snow. The seat was comfortably upholstered with smart, plush black leather with a velvet trim. Though the seat was large enough to take two or more passengers, there didn't seem to be a special bench for the driver. The studded leather reins lay coiled across the front of the sledge as if waiting for someone to take them.

Zoe thought to try the seat. She lifted a foot to climb onto the step-board but found it way too high for her. She jumped back with a tiny exclamation of surprise. The step-board was now level with the top of her head and the horse and sledge also appeared to have expanded. Now it was terrifying, enormous, and she felt like a small child looking up at the beast. What's more, the instant she moved backwards the horse, as if flicked by an unseen crop, tossed its head and trotted onwards.

'Hey!' Zoe shouted after the horse. 'Hey!'

But the stallion was already away and moving on through the gently falling flakes of snow at a steady clip, its bells shivering in a percussion of admonition. Zoe watched it go. The horse and its empty sledge rounded the curve of the road and disappeared behind a dark row of snow-burdened firs.

Zoe waited until its sound diminished and silence returned. She looked up and down the street. Then she returned to the hotel, and to the room where Jake was still sleeping.

She sat on the bed watching the gentle rise and fall of his chest as he slept on. She reached out and held his hand, half-hoping that he would wake, half-hoping that he would not. She decided to leave it to the Fates. If he woke she would tell him about the horse outside. If not, she wouldn't. She had to ask herself why she was not allowing herself to tell him about some of the events that were happening around them. Why she was staying quiet about these things was also a mystery to her. It was as if some primal part of her was terrified that no event in this place could be good for them. She felt – irrationally but with a conviction that came from deep in her bones – that with each new development, something was trying to insert itself between them. Only absolute stasis would leave them alone.

She held on to his hand. One of the first things she had noticed about him when they met was his hands. They were large and manly, but also elegant and descriptive. He used them a great deal in conversation. She wanted to be able to hold his hand for ever.

She fell asleep beside him.

12

The following evening the power failed again. They were in the lobby of the hotel when the lights flickered and went out. The lights went out over the entire village.

It had happened before, and the power had come back on after a short while. They had some candles which they lit and set on the reception desk, and waited. After an hour the power hadn't resumed so they went outside, where they could see better by the snow-charged moonlight.

The shops and restaurants were now in universal darkness. As they passed them, the individual stores had a different, sullen look to them. Snow and moonlight reflected from the dark plate glass of the shopfronts in an eerie soft blue glow.

'The power has never been off this long. What do you think it means?' Zoe asked.

Jake didn't reply and the unanswered question congealed in the cold air, following them as they trudged down the deserted main street. Their boots squeaked on the compacted snow. They had no plan: they had walked out with the expectation of the power returning at any moment. But when they reached the other end of the village, where the buildings stopped and gave way to an open tract of land that itself was swallowed up by dark woodland, the lights still hadn't come back on.

'A letter to the mayor of the village required,' Jake said, but Zoe had lost her humour. They turned and retraced their steps in silence.

Halfway back the lights flickered on all over the village and they both released an involuntary cheer. There also came the sound of generators and turbines powering up somewhere, maybe for the ski lifts they'd left switched on.

They found a wine bar and raided the banks of bottles and turned up the music system. Zoe put on 'Winter' by Tori Amos because Jake had once said that it made him want to cry but he would never allow himself to; and she asked him if he remembered where they'd first heard it.

'No,' he said, 'I can't remember.'

'Think.'

'Nope. Nothin' coming.'

So she told him. It was on one of their first ski holidays together. They'd heard it in a bar and Jake had walked up to the barman and demanded to know who had recorded the song.

'I don't remember that either.'

So she told him which holiday it was, and where, and who they were with, and who they had met.

'No, it's all a blank.'

'You must remember! Surely you do! You have to! How can you not?'

'No, I don't.'

So she described the rooms they had stayed in, where there was an old woman who had to get wood from the outhouse to feed the stove that heated the water for a bath; and how every evening she pressed her hand into her back and grimaced and shuffled out to get more

175

wood as if the request to take a shower or a bath after a day's skiing was an unreasonable one. And she told him about how their dour martinet of a ski instructor had taken them down sheets of polished ice.

He just couldn't recall any of that.

It was true that they had taken many skiing holidays together and after so many it did become difficult to distinguish some of them; but it disturbed her that he couldn't remember any of it.

'Where has it gone, that holiday?' he said. 'How come I can remember others but not that one? I mean, it's not like my memory is a DVD that fell behind the cupboard. It's just gone.'

'Doesn't matter,' she said.

'It damn well does matter. What are we if we're not the sum of our memories?'

'You're forgetting about what we might become. Isn't that more important?'

He grimaced and ran a couple of fingers through his hair, as if he were trying to locate and massage the lost holiday snaps somewhere under his skull.

'Well, you haven't forgotten this song,' she pointed out.

'No. There are certain songs, and books, and films that are like points of high ground in the memory. Like they are even larger than your own experiences. They never go away.'

'And a lot you forget.'

'Oh yes. A lot you forget.'

They stayed in the bar a while, playing music and chasing memories. Neither felt like eating so they wound their way back to their hotel, arm in arm. When they entered the reception Jake noticed something had changed.

'The candles we lit have burned down. While we were out.'

'Are they still burning down?'

'I'm not going to stand here and watch them to find out, but I wonder if they are. I mean, that would be strange, wouldn't it? If the candles were only burning down when the power was out? That would be odd, wouldn't it?'

'You know what?' she said. 'I just can't try to figure out the answer to it any more. It's driving me mad. We just have to go with the flow sometimes.'

'That would be too easy.'

'Come on. Bed,' she said.

Zoe woke up in the night feeling cold. The rooms tended to overheat, so they always left a window ajar, even though Zoe was the only one who experienced fluctuations in the temperature. She got out of bed and closed it, but as she looked out she saw that the power had gone off yet again. The lights were off all over the village. She shivered and crawled back under the duvet.

She couldn't get back to sleep. She thought about waking Jake to tell him the power had gone off again, but decided to let him sleep on. After all, there was nothing he could to do about the situation. She lay awake, her eyes open, looking up into the darkness. Maybe her restlessness pulled him out of his sleep, because she heard him whisper.

'You awake?'

She turned to look at him. His eyes were oily black pools in the darkness. 'Yes. The power is out again.'

'How long?'

'Don't know. At least an hour. I was cold. I had to close the window. Are you cold?'

'Come here. Snuggle up. Try to go back to sleep.'

In the morning they woke to learn that the power had not returned during the night. Zoe said she felt a difference in temperature: that the normally overheated hotel had cooled in the night. Jake said he couldn't feel any difference, but they were forced to discuss what might happen if the lack of power became permanent. They called it the 'energy crisis'. They discussed food supplies. The freezers in their own hotel and the supermarket and presumably all the other hotels were stocked with frozen food so they'd never had to think about where they might take food from. But if the freezers stopped working, all those supplies would rot within a few days. Unless of course they took it all outside and buried it under snow.

The hotel had a large fireplace in the lobby area. They would have to burn wood to stay warm, they decided. There was plenty of it. Jake said they could even burn the other hotels timber by timber if they ran short. Zoe put her hand on her belly. She feared the future in this place.

They went down to the lobby to check out the fireplace. The scorch marks in the hearth indicated that it was a functioning fireplace, not a decorative one, even though it didn't seem to have been used in a while. Jake proposed they go outside and look for log piles that they could drag into the reception.

It was he who noticed that the candles they had lit and placed on the reception desk had burned right down.

White wax had spilled across the polished beechwood. 'Remember those eternal flames?' he said. 'They're not eternal any more.'

'It frightens me,' she said. 'What does it mean?'

'It means the rules here are changing all the time. Come on, let's get some wood.'

About a hundred metres from the hotel was an ancient dwelling constructed from blue-grey stone with timber balconies and shutters. It might have been one of the village's original farm buildings from the days before leisure skiing changed everything. Its weathered timbers were of great age, split and greyed and grained, and there was a precarious wooden lean-to propped at the side of the house. Beneath the lean-to was a supply of neatly stacked logs under a tarpaulin. Jake spread the tarp on the ground and they began heaping logs on it so they could drag them back to the hotel.

'Such a neat pile of logs. We ought to thank whoever lived here for all their hard work.'

Zoe stopped moving logs. 'I want to look inside.'

Jake continued to heap logs onto the tarp. 'I'm not sure about that.'

'What difference can it make?'

While they had raided any available hotel, store, wine bar or restaurant they felt like, they had hitherto kept away from all private dwellings. Perhaps it was a mark of respect. Perhaps they were keeping alive a foolish hope that one day someone might come back to these houses, that the village might sometime be repopulated. Whatever it was, it had not occurred to them that they might enter a private family home.

'I want to know who lived here,' Zoe said.

Jake filled his arms with logs while she made her way around the back of the house.

The back door was not locked. Zoe turned the handle and stepped inside. She resisted the temptation to call out, to announce herself.

The interior of the house was quite dark. The door opened onto a kitchen, which itself expanded into a neat dining room, with old chairs drawn up around a table. To the right was a further room, which she took to be some kind of workshop. The house was cold, and there was a smell of damp plaster and another odour that she took to be the naphthalene of mothballs.

The room had an open fireplace with a mantelpiece and above the mantelpiece a mirror. Brass candlesticks with new candles still in cellophane stood at either end of the mantelpiece. There were matches, so Zoe stripped the cellophane from the candles and lit them. She looked at her face in the mirror.

The silver amalgam on the mirror had misted and peeled in places and rusted in pinprick holes. The mirror must have hung there for over a hundred years. The light gave her a jaundiced look, and the rusting mirror loaned her some freckles. It was unflattering. She looked rather gaunt. The fireplace beneath the mantelpiece was full of ash. She bent down to touch it, looking for warmth, but it was damp and cold.

There were two old leather armchairs drawn up on either side of the fire, with lace doilies thrown across the back of them. The doilies had a shadow where heads had rested against them over the years. She could almost smell the sebum of the chairs' occupants.

Framed photographs from two or three generations hung on the wall, the heavy wooden frames of the traditional photographic studies at odds with the chrome and plastic framed smaller pictures offering almost careless modern snapshots. Zoe could guess at the familial relationships, with a few 1970s colour shots – their photochemicals unfixing and fading – unable to compete with the vivid modern colour pictures of children.

It occurred to her that some of the people in the photos were the dead and some were the living and yet she felt equally divided from all of them.

A clock with its pendulum visible behind a glass case hung on the wall, its hands arrested at 8.50 a.m., which Zoe calculated could have been the exact time of the avalanche. She opened the case and swung the pendulum to reactivate the clock. The pendulum swayed back and forth several times with a sequence of reassuring clicks, but it died off. She tried again, but it died off again. She looked for a key, to wind the clock. It seemed important to her for a moment. Then she gave up.

She drifted from the kitchen to the workshop at the side of the house. There was a pleasing smell of wood shavings. She saw an orderly row of woodworking tools – chisels, planes, saws. Then she saw what the craftsman had been working on.

It was a coffin. The wood was still in its natural form – worked and precisely jointed, planed to a smooth finish but unveneered, waiting to be lined on the inside, dressed with handles outside and closed with a lid. She was fascinated and horrified. She stepped over to the coffin, half-expecting it to contain an embalmed corpse, but it was empty.

She heard someone come into the house. She turned smartly, and there was Jake framed in the doorway between the workshop and the living room. His face was in shadow but his eyes were swimming.

'He was a coffin maker. The man who lived here. That was his trade.'

He peered into the coffin. 'It's about my size.' Jake swung a leg up onto the workbench.

'Don't!'

He ignored her, stepping into the coffin and lowering himself to lie in it.

'I'm going out,' Zoe said and she rushed outside, leaving him to his morbid game.

Outside she waited by the tarpaulin with its load of logs. He was a long time, but she wouldn't go back inside after him. Finally he came out and without a word he grabbed a corner of the tarp and began to drag it.

Zoe took another corner of the tarp. 'That wasn't funny.'

He snorted. 'Yes it was. Was and is. It's funny.'

'No, it's not. You think you're being funny but you're not.'

'But it is funny. It's very funny.'

'No it's not.'

'Yes it is.' And he let go a peal of unforced laughter, to show her how funny it was; and the ricochet of his laughter hung in the freezing air like a cruel spectre.

Zoe compressed her lips.

When they got back to the hotel, they found that the power had returned. But within ten minutes it went off again.

'You have to laugh sometimes,' Jake said in the darkness. 'Remember my dad? You just have to. Laugh, I mean.'

13

Jake's acquaintance with death had been very different from Zoe's. When he first arrived at the hospital he found that his father had been given a private room at the end of the ward. His father, Peter, looked pretty weak, but he managed to lift his head from the pillow and blink at Jake.

'Thank God you made it, Jake. These fucking clowns have no idea. I want an armed man posted on every door. You got that?'

'It's taken care of, Dad. It's all in hand.'

Peter let his head sink back on the pillow. 'Thank fuck you got here, that's all.'

Jake had never heard his father swear before in his life. He'd heard him angry, critical, dismayed and occasionally made buoyant by a glass or two of cognac but he'd never heard him swear, cuss, or even blaspheme throughout his childhood or his mature life. Peter disapproved of swearing.

Which was difficult for Jake, because his days at university had given him a taste for a cocktail of the sacred and the profane. Hardcore swearing and blaspheming. He liked to say Jesus Fucking H. Christ without ever knowing what the 'H' stood for. He liked to say Holy Cunting Moses. One time a cupboard door at his father's home was hanging loose and while Jake was fixing it the screwdriver slipped and gashed his hand and he'd screamed Cunt the Fucking Pharisee, which as an ex-Sunday School boy and one-time chorister he himself had found both strong and surprising.

His father, who had stood back watching, merely blinked and then walked out of the kitchen.

After a moment Jake had followed him, finding him in the living room, tight-lipped and running the Hoover over the carpet. Jake switched off the Hoover at the plug and showed Peter the wound on his hand.

'What do you expect me to say? Oh Jehovah?'

'Not even that.'

'It's just words!'

'Having the cupboard door hanging off its hinges is rather less ugly than hearing that sort of language.'

'Dad, you were in the war! You were in Special Ops! You saw men spill their guts! Surely you know what is important and what isn't!'

Peter rarely leaked body language, any more than he did 'bad' language. He was a master of control. The only time he might inadvertently express surprise, irritation or pleasure would be a reflex in which he would reach up and pinch the right lens-frame of his glasses between thumb and index finger, as if to somehow increase the magnification of the lens. He did so now. 'Does it ever occur to you that that might be the very reason why I don't approve of coarse language in the house?'

Jake had thrown up his hands. In the house, out of the house. When going to visit Peter you always felt you should have taken off your shoes at the door: sooner or later you would be made to feel you had trailed something nasty in with you.

If Jake hung around long enough his father might

take a bottle of cognac out of the sideboard and pour two rather meagre splashes into heavy, large brandy balloons. Jake always wanted to ask: why have such a big glass for such a small measure? Having a glass of cognac with his father was like being invited to have a drink with the Housemaster on the day it came to leave school. He would ask what your plans were and pretend to be interested and listen with an approximation of a smile until you were done.

Peter and Jake's mother had divorced when he was twelve and his mother had gone to live in Scotland. The age gap between them – alluring and attractive to her when she'd met and married him – was a trial in later years. Ultimately she had been relieved to leave behind an aging husband. Jake had been sent to boarding school, something Zoe never let him forget, and which he couldn't anyway.

That time after the screwdriver incident they sipped their ritual brandy and just as Jake was about to put down his glass and say his farewells, Peter had opened up about bad language.

'I know it's different for your generation, but I am offended by it. I don't like it when you blaspheme, since that offends my faith; and I don't like it when you cuss because that represents a decline in values.'

'Yes, but what values, Dad?'

'You don't understand. Speaking, talking – language, that is – represents the most orderly, civilised and rational expression of human nature. All this foul-mouthed cussing is a gap where you can't think of anything to say. It's the opposite of being rational and ordered. The very opposite. It wants to unpick civilised behaviour, rationality and order.'

'Yep. I just don't happen to believe in rationality and order very much.'

'Oh! You think we should give up? Let everything slide into the sewer?'

'Not at all. What I mean is we are rational some of the time, but not all the time. We've no idea what's under the rationality. Foul language as you call it is an expression of that.'

'Ah! So we agree on one thing! It's a call to the unconscious, to death and to ordure.'

'Isn't that what's underneath everything?'

Peter sneered behind the lip of his brandy glass. 'You don't know the first thing about death, sonny. Not the first thing.' Then he admonished himself. 'I'm sorry, that was unmanly of me.'

'Unmanly? Dad! Loosen up a bit, will you? Look, swearing: it's just letting off a bit of steam. A safety valve.'

'We won't agree on that.'

Jake stood up. The time had come to leave. They always shook hands, firmly and with eye contact: his father had taught him that one should always make eye contact when shaking hands. Jake had watched Zoe and Archie hug affectionately on meeting and departing. He had wondered if resistance to the embrace was a male thing, but after a couple of years Archie was happy to offer him a hug, too. Meanwhile he and Peter had got through the years with firm handshakes and they weren't about to start hugging now.

And yet now that he saw his father lying on the hospital bed he wanted to hug him. This father who suddenly,

186

inexplicably and contrary to a lifetime of restraint had started swearing.

Peter lifted his head from the pillow. 'You know they got Charlie, don't you? Poor fucker.'

'Charlie?'

'We lost him. I'm sad about that. Good fellow in a scrap. Did you see that escarpment where we came in?'

'Escarpment?'

'Christ, I've been through this enough times. There's an overhang above the cave high in the rock. If we've got a man spare we want one stationed there all the time. Right fucking there.'

'Dad—'

'I'm not fucking well discussing it. This isn't the village fucking hall. Just see to it. I'm going to have to tell Charlie's fucking wife when we get back. If we get back. All because of a bit of cunt, I ask you.'

Jake had brought grapes and lemon barley water. He placed them on the cabinet.

'Grapes?' Peter said. 'Where in hell did you get those this time of year?'

'The supermarket, Dad.'

Peter reached up to squeeze his lens-frame, but his glasses were folded and lying on the same cabinet. He was about to say something when the ward sister walked in and picked up his chart from the clip at the foot of the bed.

'I want this place cleared of all these fucking whores.'

'Now now, Mr Bennett,' said the ward sister firmly. 'We'll have a bit less of that.'

'Get the bitch out of here, Jake. Do you know, if the army made soldiers' boots from cunt leather they would never wear out.'

'I'm sorry, I'm really sorry,' Jake said. 'Can I have a word?'

Jake stepped outside the private room with the ward sister and closed the door on Peter. 'Look, I've never heard him say such things.'

The sister was a burly woman with large bovine eyes and a bleach-blond curl spilling over her brow. 'Oh, for goodness' sake, I've heard worse than that.'

'Really? I haven't!'

'Well. You know.'

'It's like he's time-tripping. He's back in the war. It's like he's still fighting it. Is it the medication?'

'Not really. The bone cancer has caused the bone to crumble and get into his bloodstream. The calcium runs to the brain. He's not always like that. Most of the time he's very sweet.'

'That's a relief. Look, I've got a bottle of brandy in my bag and a paper cup. I know you're not supposed to, but ... is it all right if he has some?'

'I haven't seen anything.'

'Thanks.'

Nurses and soldiers, thought Jake. *They see it all, and pretend they've seen nothing.*

Peter had been a soldier on Special Operations in the war. An officer in the elite SAS force, he had commanded Operation Pepino behind enemy lines in the mountains of northern Italy during the winter of 1944–45. Thirty-two men were parachuted in in broad daylight. Their instructions were to make themselves highly visible and simulate the actions of a much larger company to divert enemy troops who were preventing an Allied advance. The operation was successful and the Germans unwittingly diverted thousands of troops.

It was a fierce winter and there was close-combat fighting with both Italian blackshirts and German troops. Peter brought back eighteen of the thirty-two men, or, as he always put it another way – lost fourteen good men. Somehow, he was back there now, in the snow-covered Italian mountains.

Jake returned to the room. His father seemed to be sleeping now. Jake took the brandy out of his bag along with two paper cups and placed them on the cabinet. Then he sat down in the plastic chair next to the bed, his hands on his knees, watching his father sleep.

After five minutes, Peter opened his eyes and said, 'You should contact your Uncle Harold. I loaned him a couple of thousand, years ago. You should have it. I've no need for it, but you should have it.'

'Harold's been dead a long time, Dad. A long time.'

Peter lifted his head from the pillow. 'Really?'

'Fifteen years.'

'Good lord. No one tells me anything. I doubt if we shall get that back.'

'Let it go, Dad.'

Peter wrinkled his nose. 'I'll have a grape.'

'I've washed them,' Jake said. 'You've no need to worry about that.' He handed his father the grapes.

Peter lay back, feeding the grapes to himself, chewing them very slowly while gazing up at the ceiling. Perhaps twenty minutes went by. Then at last Peter said, 'Where's Charlie? I'm worried to death about Charlie.'

'Charlie's gone, Dad.'

'Gone? He was here a moment ago.'

'Dad, listen. You're in hospital.'

'What?'

'Warwick Hospital. You're getting treatment for your cancer and you're going to be well.'

'What?'

'Zoe is coming to see you with me tomorrow.'

'Zoe? Zoe's your wife.'

'That's right.'

Peter dragged himself upright. It was a struggle and his face contorted as he pulled himself up. Then he looked around the room, as if seeing it for the first time. 'I've got cancer.'

'Yes, Dad. But you're doing well.'

'Liar.'

'You're doing good. I was just speaking with the ward sister. Look, I brought you a drop of cognac. The good stuff.'

'Cognac. You are a star, son. A star.'

Jake stood up and poured two – this time generous – measures of cognac into the paper cups. He handed one of the cups to his father, who took a healthy gulp. Then the door swung open.

A middle-aged lady with close-cropped hair bounced into the room wielding a clipboard in one hand and rapidly clicking a ballpoint in the other. She wore a tight-fitting dark suit slashed by a wide crimson belt. There was an almost pantomime energy in the mobility of her face. 'Hell-o, hell-o! How are we today?'

'We're fine,' said Jake. 'Thanks.'

'That's really great and fabulous,' she said, 'because I'm taking requests for WHR.'

'Requests?'

'Who the fuck are you?' Peter bellowed at her. 'Who the fuck let you in here?'

The mobility drained from the lady's face. She

over-focused on Jake. 'WHR. Warwick Hospital Radio. I'm making a request list and we'll play the requests this evening.'

'You insufferably silly cunt!'

Jake said, 'My dad kind of likes Sinatra. Stuff like that.'

Peter shouted, 'Do you know the song "Me and You in a Lead Canoe"? No? Me fucking neither. You should be buried in a Y-shaped coffin. Cunt!'

'His name is Peter Bennett and he'd like "Love Is the Tender Trap".'

The lady wrote it down carefully. 'Love. Is. The. Tender Trap. I like that one. Well, that's really great and fabulous! I'll leave you boys to it!'

Peter had his glasses on now and he was squeezing the lens-frame and wrinkling his nose in disdain at the lady in the red belt.

'Thanks,' said Jake. 'He'll enjoy that.'

Peter said quietly after she'd gone, 'Never mind that twatting whore, come over here. I want to tell you something. Come closer.'

Jake leaned in towards the bed. Peter beckoned him still closer. He wanted to whisper something. He pressed his thumb and his forefinger together. 'We're out of supplies. There isn't going to be another drop. No. Our only chance is to get across the mountain.'

'You know—'

'Shut it and listen. We'll dump the Bren guns and the ammo with the partisans. The Krauts will think we're still here. Charlie's got gangrene and he can't even move. I love the bloke – none finer – but you know what I'm going to have to do.'

'No, Dad.'

'No other way, son, no other way.'

Jake watched his father grind his teeth. Peter lay back twisting his fingers together. He was clearly in a state of anguish.

Jake cleared his throat. 'Dad. I'll take care of that for you.'

'What?'

'Charlie. I'll deal with it.'

'No. Not having that. Absolutely fucking not. I'm the CO around here and I'm the one who has to do it.'

'I'm going to take care of it for you.'

'No you won't and *that's an order*. My responsibility. Not yours.' Peter eyeballed him and perhaps for the first time ever, Jake realised what a ferocious and determined figure was his father.

'You can't move,' Jake said at last. 'You're laid up here. I'm going to do it with or without your permission.'

'Don't even think about it, sonny. Don't even think about it.'

'I'm going out of that door right now and I'm going to do it.'

Peter raged. Ignoring his father's protests and all the obscenities that went with them Jake got up, went out of the room and closed the door. From behind the door he heard his father roaring, *Come back here, you little shit*, and the rest. Jake vented a deep sigh and ran both hands through his hair. A pretty nurse at the desk looked up at him. He folded his arms and stood with his back to the closed door for about three minutes.

Then he went back inside. His father had calmed down. He looked at Jake expectantly.

'It's done,' said Jake.

'I didn't hear a shot.'

'I muffled it. Charlie's dead. It's all taken care of.'

Peter removed his spectacles and pinched the bridge of his nose. 'Bloody good man. One of the best of us.' Then he looked around the room again; and at the bottle of brandy that stood on the cabinet; and at the grapes; and finally at Jake. 'Jake, what the hell are you doing here?'

'I'm visiting you, Dad.'

'But you shouldn't be here. This isn't right. You shouldn't be— God, I'm so confused. So confused.'

There was a tremble in his voice; a tremble Jake had never heard before. It was the first sign of emotional frailty he'd ever witnessed in his father and it lacerated his heart. He got up and made to hug him, but Peter seemed almost repelled by the advance. Instead he half-hugged him, and broke the hug by pretending he was straightening the pillow and rearranging the sheets.

'Where's Zoe?' Peter said.

'Oh! She's coming tomorrow.'

'I want to see my Zoe. Lovely girl. I want to see her.'

'Sure thing, Dad. She'll be along tomorrow.'

'He asked for you today.' Jake told Zoe that evening.

'By name? He can't be that bad if he asked for me by name.'

Jake had told her all about Peter's delusions that he was back in the Italian mountains. 'He's time-tripping. He's in and out.'

'Why do you think he's back there in particular?'

Jake shook his head. 'Probably the most stressful time of his life. Plus there's guilt. He had to kill one of his own men.'

'He told you that?'

'It came out. I'm not sure you should go tomorrow. He was okay with me but every time a female walked into the room he went fucking crazy. I mean, the air was blue.'

'I can handle that.'

'No, like angry-blue. Out-of-control blue.'

'I have to come with you. Anyway, he asked for me, didn't he? I have to.'

They went back together the following evening. The nurse at the desk told them that Peter had had an uncomfortable day. When they went in, Jake thought he sensed a miasma, a cloudiness in the room he hadn't detected the previous evening. Peter at first appeared to be asleep but then he opened his eyes.

'It's looking bleak,' Peter said.

Jake didn't know whether he was referring to the cancer or to his chances in the mountains. 'You're a fighter, Dad,' he said. 'You've always been a fighter.'

Peter seemed to consider that.

Zoe approached him. 'Hello, Dad.' She always called him 'Dad', just like Archie, and Peter had always liked it.

'Zoe,' he said, accepting a kiss. 'I so wanted to see you.'

'Well, I'm here. How are you feeling?'

'Lot of pain. Comes through the morphine, it does. And sometimes I don't know where I am. And I want to cry. But we're not having that, are we?'

'I doubt it,' said Zoe. She sat on the edge of the bed and stroked his hair. 'Well. We're here for you now.'

'Never mind that. I had something important to say

to you but it's gone clean out of my head. What use is that?'

They waited in silence as he tried to remember.

Then Jake sat down in the plastic chair and said, 'Did you tune in to hospital radio last night?'

'What?'

'They had a request for you. Frank Sinatra. Played it for you specially.'

Peter looked at Zoe and laughed, though the laugh pained him. 'He's barking mad, isn't he? What on earth is he talking about? I don't know how you ever came to marry him.'

'It's a mystery, Dad,' she said.

'Oh, that was it: I remembered what I wanted to say. Hang on to him, for his sake. Death us do part and all that. Hang on to him. You've been the making of that boy. You really have.'

'Oh?'

'That was it. And to ask you for one thing. One little hug. From you. One little hug.'

'I can do that, Peter.'

Zoe inched up the bed as far as she was able and put her arms around him and laid her face against the rough stubble of his cheek. Jake watched from the plastic chair. The hug lasted for ten or twelve seconds, during which Peter flicked a finger at Zoe's hair.

'That's enough,' he said.

'Do I get a hug?' Jake asked.

'Unmanly.'

'Okay.'

Peter didn't have a lot of chat left in him. Zoe and Jake both exhausted themselves trying to initiate conversations, dredging up bits of news in which he might be interested. But the time-slip seemed to have released him from its claws, and for that Jake felt grateful. He didn't want to have to go outside to put a bullet through Charlie a second time.

Peter fell asleep after a while, and they left. The hospital would inform them if there was any change in his condition. Zoe drove on the way home.

'Did you smell it?' Jake asked her as she drove.

'Smell what?'

'Maybe nothing.'

They got home and before Jake put the key in the door he heard the phone ringing. It was the hospital calling to say that Peter had slipped away in the last hour.

14

Jake was at the window of their hotel room.

'What are you looking at?' Zoe wanted to know.

'Nothing.'

She stepped forwards to see for herself, but he turned quickly and blocked her advance towards the window. She giggled, and tried to slip by him. He blocked her again.

'What are you doing?'

He said nothing. Just held her so that she couldn't get to the window. She tried to push his arms away from her, but he bear-hugged her, steering her towards the bed, finally toppling her backwards onto it.

'Get off me, Jake! I want to see.'

She pushed him away and struggled to her feet, rushing to the window. She looked out across the snow. The sky presaged more in heavy grey clouds. The road curved away into the distance, flanked on either side by trees like frozen sentries in a forgotten war. There was nothing she hadn't seen before.

Jake came up behind her, peering over her shoulder. He reached an arm around her belly, stroking her.

'What was it?' she demanded to know.

'Nothing.'

'You lie.'

'Yes.'

'So tell me.'

'No.'

Something made her shiver. She turned suddenly and grabbed his jaw with her hand, squeezing. 'Are you protecting me? I don't want to be protected. Whatever there is to be known about this place, I want you to tell me.'

He took her hand away from his mouth. 'It was a horse.'

'A horse?'

'Yes, a horse. And a sledge. It was waiting there. Now it's gone.'

'Why didn't you tell me?'

'I've seen it there before. It frightened me.'

'What do you mean? You've seen it before?'

'Yes. A few times.'

'I saw it too.'

'What? You saw it? You saw the horse and you didn't tell me?'

'Yes. A huge black horse with a red plume, pulling an enormous sledge.'

'How could you not tell me? Zoe, what were you thinking?'

'Can you hear yourself? A moment ago you wouldn't even let me look out of the window.'

He shook his head and sank onto a chair. 'All right. Let's make a promise. Let's not try to protect each other. In this place. I mean it.'

Jake was astonished to learn that Zoe had stolen out into the night, and had stood next to the steaming horse; that she had stroked its flanks and had even tried to get onto the sledge. She told him that the horse and sledge were huge, but that when she'd tried to climb onto the sledge it had swollen massively without warning; or perhaps she had suddenly shrunk, like Alice.

They decided to go out and look at the place where the horse had stood.

There were tracks in the snow, left by the runners on the sledge and the horse's hooves. There was also some dung.

'Well, that shows it was real,' Jake said, 'but just look at this stuff.'

He picked up some of the dung in his ski glove and offered it for her to see.

'Nice. Thanks.'

'Look at it.'

It was the shape and texture of ordinary horse dung. But it rippled with iridescent light. It sparkled. It shimmered blue, green, red and violet; swirling with its own light.

'Are we dreaming?' Zoe said. 'Is it a trick of the light?'

'It's not.'

But even as Jake held it in his glove, the sparkling dung faded, crumbled, turned to sand, disappeared. The rest of the dung on the snow vanished too, and so did the hoof-prints and the tramline impressions left behind by the sledge's runners.

'And I was just about to suggest we follow the tracks,' Jake said.

'Jake, we haven't tried for a while.'

'Tried what?'

'Just to walk out.'

'No.'

'Why haven't we?'

'Because we're in a place where a horse shits rainbows.'

'Right.'

They went back to the hotel. Neither the lighting nor the heating had returned and the temperature was dropping rapidly now. It was astonishing how quickly a hotel of that size could discharge its heat. Jake remembered he had found an axe embedded in a log at the house they'd raided. He said he was going out to chop kindling. He said that if they needed to, they would sleep in front of the fire.

While he was out Zoe swept and prepared the fireplace for his return. In a nook in the stone surround she found a set of playing cards. She took them out. They were some kind of Tarot cards. Zoe had seen packs of such cards before and this was some continental version with the Major Arcana titles in French. Most of the major cards were the same as the standard Tarot deck, *La Lune*, *Le Soleil* and such, but some were different. There was a card called *La Montagne*, the mountain, and another depicting a compass, perhaps instead of the conventional Wheel of Fortune. Another card was *Le Chien* and she didn't remember a dog card from the Tarot. She found another card that made her catch her breath.

It was a depiction of two large black birds, each perched on one of the posts either side of a gate. It brought to mind the two large crows she had encountered on the morning when she had returned to the stranded police car. She shivered.

She began slowly sorting through the cards, looking for the Death card. Her hand slowed as she turned each card, knowing that it was in there somewhere. Then she decided that whatever it looked like, she didn't want to see it. She gathered up the cards and returned them to the nook in the fireplace where she'd found them.

When Jake returned with his kindling she helped him to build a fire. They got it ready for the match, but didn't light it. Of the cards she said nothing.

The food laid out on the kitchen workspace had rotted. Jake cleared it away. He had watched it like you would watch a clock; but now he had unpleasant thoughts about maggots and decomposition, so he scraped it all into a plastic bin-bag and took the bag out behind the hotel. He wiped down the workspace with bleach.

There was now no power, neither electric nor gas, on which to cook. So they found cheese and biscuits and fruit. Plus of course a very fine bottle of red wine. It occurred to him that they would run out of food long before they ran out of wine.

'We'll never run out of sin,' he said while drawing the cork from a bottle.

'What?'

'I said we'll never run out of wine.' He handed her a glass. 'Here.'

'No you didn't. You said we'll never run out of sin.'

'Wine. I said wine.'

'No you didn't. You said sin. You said we'll never run out of sin.'

'I did?'

'Yes.'

'Must have been a slip of the tongue.'

'Yes. Are you going to light the fire?'

So he lit it, and they watched intently as the flames licked at the kindling, like it was a programme of entertainment with the outcome uncertain. But the flame ate the kindling and Jake put smaller logs on the fire, and the flames grabbed at the logs like fingers rolling them into a devouring mouth. Then he laid bigger logs in its path and pretty soon the fire was roaring in the chimney breast.

Twilight fell like a mantle, a quiet invasion, a horde of creeping creatures surrounding the hotel. Jake dragged a couple of mattresses from the nearest hotel rooms and went back for duvets while Zoe placed and lit candles all around the reception desk and the lobby. Outside, the twilight plumped itself into darkness.

Jake watched without comment as Zoe bolted the hotel side door. As for the plate-glass doors of the lobby, she took a pair of decorative antique skis from the wall and inserted them through the door handles, barricading the door.

'Who do you think is coming?' Jake said with a half-smile.

'No one.'

'The Devil?'

'No.'

'God?'

'No.'

'Something else?'

'Shut up. I just feel better with it all locked and secure, okay?'

They drank two bottles of wine. Jake kept the fire stoked with logs. Zoe settled under the duvets and gazed into the flames. She saw shapes there. She fell asleep.

In the night she heard men. They were tramping around the hotel. She heard their voices. She heard the sound of their boots squeaking and stamping on the snow. They called softly to each other. She was unable to understand what they were saying, and neither could she get up to look out of the window. She was paralysed both by terror of the men outside and by the half-sleep that had folded her in its arms. When she tried to rise she felt unable to move. It was as if she were drugged. She was unable to stir a hand or a foot. She was unable to blink. She couldn't speak or call out to Jake, because her lips and her jaw were clamped shut. All she could do was gaze into the fire, and witness the blurred shifting of burning logs.

15

When they woke up the fire had gone out. It was impossible to see anything from the windows of the hotel because a thick mist had descended on the valley, bringing with it fresh snow. Zoe stood at the plate-glass doors of the lobby, huddled in her duvet. The doors were still barred by the ancient skis. She debated whether to tell Jake about the men walking around the hotel in the night.

She was still protecting him, just as he was trying to protect her. But from what? From what? They were already counted among the dead. What could possibly threaten them?

She heard him stir behind her. Without looking around, she said, 'There were men, in the night. Walking round and round the hotel. Unless I was dreaming. But if I was dreaming it was the first dream I've had here.'

He came up behind her. He sniffed and put a hand on her shoulder. 'I heard them, too.'

She turned quickly, her eyes flaring. 'You did?'

He slid the old skis out from behind the handles of the glass doors and leaned them against the wall. Then he dressed quickly.

'You're not going out there.'

'I am.'

'I don't want you to. What did you hear? In the night, what did you hear?'

'I heard some men pacing around the place.'

'How do you know they were men?' she said, and now there was a tremble in her voice.

'Well, I don't. But I heard their footfalls and it sounded like men. I heard their breathing. I heard a cough, too.'

'Did they try to get in?'

'I don't think so. I think they came right up to the window but they didn't try to get in.'

'What if it's not men?'

'What would it be, if it were not?'

'What if it were demons?'

He snorted with derision. 'You don't believe in demons.'

'Maybe I do now. I don't want you to go out there.'

Jake stamped his feet into his boots and laced them up in silence. 'We can't stay in here for ever, that's for sure. I'm not going to be a prisoner. If there are men out there, I want to find out what they are doing. And if they are demons, well, I want to see what they look like. Are you coming?'

He held out his hand for her. She didn't budge.

'They can't hurt us.'

'They can.'

'Zoe! We died! Some time ago we died in an avalanche! What can they do to us? What can they possibly do? Kill us again?'

She blinked. She knew exactly what they could do. Something Jake didn't understand. But she didn't say it. She just said, 'Wait.'

She dressed hurriedly, pulling on the boots and ski jacket she had liberated from those deserted stores. He waited patiently; then, when she was ready he held the door open, and they stepped outside.

The icy cold clawed at them. Visibility was less than a few metres. The damp mist was in their faces and the fog of it was in their throats. Snow was coming down hard in small flakes.

They walked around the hotel, looking for boot-prints made by the men in the night; or if not boot-prints, then any kind of tracks that might suggest the nature of whatever had been out there. Or what might still be out there. But there were no boot-prints, nor claw-prints, nor tracks of any kind. They had presumably disappeared in the same way as those hoof-prints and tramlines left behind by the horse and its giant sledge.

But Jake did find something.

He held it up for her. It was a cigarette butt. The filter had been bent as if twisted between the fingers as it was put out. There were more. Every few yards they found another. They discussed how long the cigarette butts might have been there; how fresh they seemed; whether the residual tobacco smelled stale, whether the paper looked pristine and chalky white or weathered and grey. They discussed whether they had spotted the cigarette butts in the snow before that moment; they couldn't be certain. Perhaps they had been there all along, and it was only now, after the presence of intruders, that they had spotted them. They sniffed the stubs, opened out and spread the remnants of paper, crushed the tobacco between their fingers. They pored over the discarded butts like they were the Dead Sea Scrolls, papyrus writings in an inaccessible language, all the time looking for meaning, meaning, meaning.

Then, behind the hotel, Zoe spotted another cigarette butt in which a single burning cinder of tobacco glinted and went out. A miraculously thin wisp of smoke floated upwards from the cigarette butt. She reached down and plucked it up, blew on it and it sparked.

She held the stub of cigarette at arm's length for Jake to see and he gazed back at it with appalled eyes.

Zoe turned and shouted into the swirling mist. 'Hello! Hello! Who is there?'

But her words were muffled by the freezing fog, seeming to fall back with a clatter at her feet.

Jake made a megaphone of his hands. 'Hellooooooooo!' he bellowed. But his voice didn't carry. 'We know you are there!' he shouted. Then he turned to Zoe. 'No we don't,' he said quietly.

They both peered deep into the mist, and Zoe saw, or thought she saw, a tiny spark, crimson-to-gold, perhaps the glowing ember of the tip of a burning cigarette as it was inhaled by the smoker. But it was so small, and the flare was so brief, that she couldn't be certain.

Perhaps Jake saw it too, because he set off into the mist, weaving slightly, as if targeted on some point in the middle distance. He hadn't gone more than a dozen steps before his outline began to fade. Unable to conceal the panic in her voice, Zoe summoned him back.

'I'm just going to take a look around.'

'I'm afraid! You might lose your way back.'

'No I won't.'

'Jake, you asked me what they could do that was worse than dying. I'm going to tell you. They could separate us.'

'What?'

'They could separate us.'

Jake hesitated, staring back at her. He seemed not to have considered this possibility. He returned to her side and hugged her to him. 'I won't let them do that. Let's go back inside.'

They returned to the hotel, and once inside Zoe made to reinsert the antique skis through the door-handles, but Jake gently took the skis out of her hands and laid them aside. Suddenly she shivered. Her teeth started to chatter, like when she had the flu. Jake found the duvet and settled it around her shoulders.

'You're freezing,' he said. 'I'll light the fire again.'

'Are you not cold?'

He shook his head, no. He'd never felt the cold all the time they had been in this place. But her teeth chattered, and she shook. Jake got down on his knees before the fire and struck a match. It sparked and hissed and in a few moments he had the fire going again and was banking it up with smaller logs. Then he cleared the area so she could sit before the comforting flames.

'These logs don't last long,' he said. 'I'm going to have to go out there at some point and get some more.'

'I wish you wouldn't.'

'Look, it's about a hundred paces up the gradient of the road. Even in this mist I can't get lost out there. And the way you're shaking, we're going to have to feed that fire.'

'I can't help it.'

'Tell you what, I'll take the tarp and drag another load of logs back here. And after that I will make you a breakfast, cooked over the fire in a skillet, old-style. Won't that be great?'

'Take the tarp. Skillet.'

'What?'

She blinked at him. She didn't feel at all hungry. 'Could we have the breakfast first? Before you go out?'

He smiled. 'Sure.' He sidled over to her and pulled the duvet around her shoulders and put his arm around her, trying to pass on some of his warmth. He held her tight but he seemed to drift off somewhere, deep in his own thoughts.

Her shivering had subsided. She could feel the heat of the fire now. She looked at Jake. 'You okay?'

'Yes. Why?'

'You look—'

'I was just about to do something and I couldn't remember what it was.'

'You were going to cook breakfast. On a skillet. Over the fire.'

'I was?'

'Yes.'

'That's right. I was. Funny. Funny how it comes back.'

He got up and headed off towards the kitchen and she watched him go. Something about his demeanour wasn't right. She wondered if he'd taken a knock to his head during the avalanche that had affected him. His eyes still hadn't recovered from being bloodshot. It was the sort of thing you would get checked out in a hospital. But here there was no hospital, no doctor, no nurse. She didn't even know if or how much you could hurt yourself in this place. She thought about the baby growing in her belly.

Jake came back with a large, oiled frying pan, plates, bacon, eggs, bread and set about making a flat bed of the burning logs so he could heat the pan. 'The freezer has shut down. We should eat this bacon while we still can. Everything is going to decompose and after a few more days we'll be eating out of tins.'

He laid out strips of bacon on the pan. 'Hungry?'

She pretended she was.

'It's like camping,' he said.

She watched him carefully steering the pan into the flames and had to fight back tears.

They ate breakfast in silence, until he said, 'Remember it for me. Remember the taste of bacon.'

'Well. You were a vegetarian when I met you.'

'Was I?'

'I converted you.'

'Really?'

'Are you serious? You don't remember that? You must remember that!'

He looked pained. 'I seem to be forgetting so many things. I try to recall it but it's just not there. I listen to you telling me stories about things we did together, and it's as though you're talking about someone else.'

'It was a couple of months after we'd got together. We'd spent forty-eight hours in bed together at my flat. We'd only got out of bed to go as far as the toilet. It was shocking. We couldn't tear ourselves away from each other. We'd been fucking all day and all night and snoozing in between and we'd eaten nothing. And I said: right, that's it. I'm having a bacon sandwich, and you said, can't, vegetarian and all that. I said too bad please yourself and I went down to the kitchen and made a bacon roll dripping with bacon fat and tomato sauce and brought it back up and you watched me eat it, and then when I'd finished it I said too bad you can't kiss me now cos you'll get bacon fat in your mouth. Disgusting you said, that's disgusting; and then you kissed me. And you drew your head back and licked your lips and you said, right that's it.'

'I said "right that's it"?'

'You said right that's it, nine years of vegetarianism and that's an end to that, can you make me one? And I did. That's it.'

'Must have been a hell of a kiss.'

'It was. A carnal kiss. You loved it.'

'Anything else you converted me to or from?'

'You were teetotal.'

'You're joking!'

'Yes, I am about that. You really don't remember, do you?'

'Yes. No. I don't know. There's so much I seem to have forgotten.'

She was deeply worried about him but she said, 'It doesn't matter. It doesn't matter because everything you can see or touch or hear or smell has a story attached to it; a story I can tell you. If you say bacon I can tell you a story. If you say snow I can tell you a dozen different stories. This is what we are: a collection stories that we share, in common. This is what we are to each other.'

He stared hard at her, his bloodshot eyes full of love and admiration for her. Then he stood up.

'Where are you going?'

'I'm going to get some wood, to keep you warm. What we have here won't last the rest of the day, let alone the night. I'll go straight there, get the logs, and I'll come straight back.'

He bent down to kiss her and then froze and pulled back.

'What is it?'

'The taste of you. It came back.'

He kissed her again and then stood up quickly. He grabbed a corner of the tarp and flicked off the few remaining logs before rolling it under his arm. Then he went out through the lobby doors and set off into the thick mist, small flakes of snow billowing about his ears.

Zoe banked up the fire with logs and waited. She did nothing but gaze into the flames. After a while she became anxious. It felt as if Jake had been gone a long time. She took the breakfast plates and the pan away to the kitchen and washed them. When she came back to the lobby it was thronged with people.

It was the same people as before, crowding the lobby all over again. They chattered excitedly. The place was packed. People were standing in line for the reception desk, waiting to register. The three receptionists were busy all over again, one on the telephone, one processing a credit card and a third frowning and struggling to hear what her grey-suited manager was trying to say above the din. The exact scene was replicated in minute detail.

There was the sneeze of air brakes from the luxury bus. Here was the man who passed her, winking suggestively as he went by. Here was the whiff of his cologne.

It was all being repeated, all over again.

Zoe heard the word 'avalanche' mentioned by a woman at the reception desk. She looked up and her eye was caught by the bald-headed concierge, who was waving at her, beckoning her to come across the lobby to him. 'Madam!' he called. 'Madam!'

But Zoe was paralysed. She couldn't move a muscle. The scene, played before her for a third time, began to take on a menacing appearance. Even though the people looked at ease, their animation and the enthusiasm of their chatter made her bowels churn.

The concierge in his maroon and grey livery saw that she was stuck. He smiled encouragement. Then he picked up a brown envelope and waved it at her.

Zoe shook her head.

The concierge said something to another resident and started to make his way through the throng towards her, all the time waving the envelope.

'It's not for me,' Zoe said. 'It's not for me.'

'But Madam!' said the concierge as he closed in on her.

Zoe shut her eyes.

And when she opened them again, the concierge was gone, and all the other residents chattering in the lobby had gone, and the three receptionists and the English women and the bus with all its new arrivals. All had vanished.

Zoe closed her eyes once more, this time for a count of ten. When she opened them she was relieved to find the lobby still empty, still deserted. Whatever she was being shown in this repeated vision, she didn't want it. She vented a huge sigh and, still trembling from the shock of the repeated but utterly lifelike vision, went to the window and peered outside. The mist seemed to be lifting, just a little. The snow flurries had diminished, but visibility was still low.

She returned to her place in front of the fire. Then she got up again and revisited the window. She looked out, and there she saw a slight movement.

It was difficult to see anything beyond twenty or thirty metres. The mist was drifting now, with gusts of wind opening up visibility here and there for a few brief moments. But she glimpsed a grey wolf-like shape, and again a movement that suggested something was out there.

She peered hard into the mist, wishing that Jake was back. Then there was another gust of wind, and as the mist lifted she saw the men.

There were three of them. They were assembled in a group, though one of them was in a crouched position, elbow on his knee. The wolf-like shape. He was smoking a cigarette and staring back at the hotel. They were all smoking cigarettes. As the mist billowed around them, she saw the embers of a cigarette spark as one of them inhaled; and she saw the plumes of smoke as others breathed out. They all smoked and looked back at the hotel. Not at her, exactly: they hadn't spotted her. They were all smoking and gazing back at different aspects of the hotel.

She ducked her head. Her heart slapped like a piston inside her and her breath came short. She slithered to the floor. After a few moments she collected herself and crawled to another part of the window where there was a curtain, and from there she was able to use the crack between the curtain and the wall to observe the men.

But they barely moved, other than to lift their cigarettes to their mouths or to blow out smoke. One man threw his cigarette to the ground and stamped on it. A few moments later he produced a packet and got another cigarette, taking a light from one of the others. The third member of the group remained in a crouched position, scanning the hotel, always scanning.

She thought of Jake out there. He would be returning at any moment with the wood. They would see him. They would see him coming back with the wood.

She tried to still her heart. *Think*, she said to herself. *Think*. She had to find a way to warn him. Had to find a way that didn't reveal to the group of men that they were there, that they were holed-up in the hotel. She had to get to Jake and warn him.

A back way out of the hotel. Though she had never used it, there had to be a back way out of the hotel. Maybe a fire exit. Or a door from the kitchen – yes, that was it. She had seen a door from the kitchen. Jake had used it to take out the garbage. She could go out of that door and make her way around the side of the hotel. From there she could get to the road. That was it; that was what she had to do.

She hunkered down and crawled beneath the windows, hugging close to the wall. When she'd cleared the windows she was able to stand upright and make her way through the restaurant with the certainty of moving unseen. From there she stepped through the swing doors of the kitchen.

It felt even colder in the kitchen. She realised she'd left her coat by the fire.

She decided to go without her coat. She crossed the tiled kitchen floor and found the rear door unlocked. Once outside, she picked her way between the rubbish bins and the garbage skips. From there it was possible to creep silently around the side of the hotel to get to the road.

But once she drew level with the road she saw that there was a vista of maybe fifteen or twenty metres, between the hotel and the building diametrically opposite the hotel, where she would be exposed. She could see the three men, immobile, still surveying the hotel, still smoking their cigarettes. It was too far to run. They would easily spot her flitting across the street.

But as she pressed her nose against the wall, trying to keep out of sight but at the same time to spy on the men, there was another flurry of mist, almost but not completely obscuring her view of them. The mist drifted before them like smoke: now they were there, now they were not. She knew that if the mist were with her, she could race across the road unseen.

She waited for her moment. It was maddening. The mist hung in the air like a prancing unicorn or a chimera, partly obscuring her view of the men, but not fully. She could see their legs, or their covered heads, as the mist broiled this way and that. Their patience was terrifying. They simply watched, waiting, smoking.

At last the mist roiled in with a new flurry of snow and Zoe put her head down and ran. She ran in the icy snow, her feet slipping; but she recovered, launching herself to the other side of the road where the men would not be able to see her.

Panting heavily she pressed her back against the wall, steam escaping from her mouth. Then she hurried towards the house where Jake had gone to fetch the wood. It took her no more than two minutes. When she reached the now depleted log pile she found the tarpaulin heaped with logs, but no sign of Jake.

She was afraid now that if the men did leave their station they might spot her, so she went inside the house, hoping to find Jake. As before, the door opened freely onto the dark kitchen. Dull light reflected from the old mirror above the mantelpiece. Her eyes were drawn to the cabinet-maker's workshop, with its available coffin. She stepped towards the workshop and then turned suddenly to see Jake. He had his back to her and he was looking at the wall.

'Jake! There are men.'

Jake turned to face her and put a finger to his lips, to hush her. Then he turned back to the wall.

She bustled over to him. 'Three men.'

'Are you sure?' He seemed to be in a trance.

'Of course!'

'Look,' he said, unimpressed by her report. 'Look at the photographs.'

She gasped.

'How long,' Jake said, 'how long ago was it that we were here in this house?'

'It was only ... yesterday. No. Wait, that's right. It was yesterday.'

'It feels to me like such a long time since we were here. Weeks. Months.'

'No! It was only yesterday.'

Jake was still gazing at the photo frames. Where Zoe recalled the generations of families represented by formal, sepia portraits and modern, fading snapshots, there were now none. The photographs had all gone from the frames. All of the frames, whether mounted on the wall or resting on flat surfaces, were empty. It made her blood sting with cold. It made her skin prickle with heat.

'The men, Jake! There are men watching the hotel.'

He seemed utterly unafraid. 'Let's go and talk to them.'

'No! We have to get back inside the hotel!'

'I don't know about that.' He still seemed to be in a daze. There was almost a slur to his words. 'If there are men, I have to talk with them.'

Zoe slapped Jake's face, hard. 'I won't let you. I won't hear of it! You are not to go out there!'

He looked at her and smiled. Then he cupped her cheek with his hand, a tender mirroring of the mighty slap she'd given him. He turned and went out, and she followed at his heels. Outside, the mist was still so thick that visibility was back down to a few metres. He took the corner of the tarpaulin loaded with logs and began to drag it back to the hotel.

'Leave it. We don't need it.'

'We have to keep you warm,' said Jake, almost distracted. 'We have to.'

'We can go in by the back way. The kitchen door. If we can get across the road without them seeing us then we'll be fine.'

The mist was thick, and Zoe prayed they could get back to the rear of the hotel without being spotted. The tarpaulin dragged noisily against the snow in a way that she thought the men must surely be able to hear. She grabbed two corners and made Jake lift it at the other two corners so that they could carry it silently.

When they came to the exposed position, the mist was thick enough to give cover, and though she couldn't see if the men were still in position, she sensed that they were close. The tarpaulin was heavy with its load of logs and they made ungainly progress; but the distance was a short one and within a couple of minutes they were at the rear entrance of the hotel, carrying the load into the kitchen. Once inside Zoe banged the door shut and locked the security bar into place.

'Where are they?' Jake said.

'Watching the front. There are three of them and they're watching for movement.'

'I have to go and speak with them.'

'Please don't do that! Please don't!'

'I have to.'

'You don't have to, Jake! We can stay here! We're safe here! We can stay warm! We have enough food! We don't have to do anything. Please don't go out to them.'

He ignored her and set off through the kitchen, paced through the restaurant and out into the lobby area, all of the time with Zoe trying to pull him back by his sleeve. He went over to the fireplace and picked up the axe from where he'd been chopping wood. Then he made for the door. Zoe ran after him and flung herself between him and the thick glass doors of the lobby, crying, begging him not to go outside.

'Don't you see why I have to go and find out what they want? Don't you see that? Now listen. It will be fine. You can stay here, or you can come with me. But I think you should stay here and in a minute or two I will come back and tell you what they want.'

With her hand pressed to her mouth she watched him go out, walking into the mist that had become a fog, the axe gripped in his hand and swinging at his side. He stepped into the fog and was swallowed up.

Zoe stood behind the glass doors, her eyes fixed on the point of invisibility, counting the seconds. She waited a minute, two minutes perhaps, but then she couldn't bear it, she couldn't bear to watch and wait. She ran out of the doors and after him, calling his name, running through the fog, until at last she saw him, standing immobile, the axe held still at his side.

She ran to him, flinging herself at him.

'Where?' he said. 'Where were they?'

'They were right here. I swear it. Right here. One was leaning against that boulder. Another had his foot up on that rock. Look! Here's one of their cigarettes! It's still smoking. They're here, Jake, they're here!'

She picked up the smoking cigarette end and showed him. The residual tobacco sparked dimly in the freezing, swirling air.

'Well, maybe they *were* here, but they're not here now.'

Jake put the axe under his arm and cupped his hands again like a megaphone. 'Show yourselves!' he bellowed into the fog. 'Show yourselves!' But his cry had no carriage, no timbre in the freezing mist, and it crashed back to earth. He weighed the handle of his axe again in his hand and took a few steps forwards. The glacial breeze flicked at his hair and the mist went billowing.

'Don't step out of sight!' Zoe shouted to him.

But he moved a few metres forwards and to the left, scanning the smoky mist, finding nothing, moving across and almost out of her range of vision, mist coiling around him. Zoe turned to look back at the hotel. A face loomed at her, centimetres from her cheek. The mouth was partially covered by a scarf. Eyes peered from deep sockets. The breath from the gash-like mouth above the scarf congealed on her cheek.

She screamed.

She came round in front of the fire in the hotel lobby. Jake supported her neck and was trying to get her to drink the water that was spilling down her chin. She sat up, looked to right and left, still in the grip of her fear, ready to bolt.

'You passed out,' said Jake.

'I saw one of them.'

'You screamed and you passed out.'

'Did you see him?'

'No.'

'He was close enough to touch me. I could have reached out and touched him.'

'There was no one there, my love.'

'I saw him.'

'I don't know what you saw. You were certainly frightened. When you're frightened you can see or hear anything. There's no one there. I had a good look around. There's no one.'

She shivered. Her teeth chattered again.

'You're cold. I'm going to build up the fire again for you.'

She pulled the duvet around her and he drew a second one over her knees. She was shivering violently. Jake went to work straight away, splitting miraculously thin kindling with the axe, all of which he grouped amid the ashes of the fire. He lit the thin spills and expertly assembled a pyramid of larger splints around the burning wood. It all burned fast. Soon the fire was roaring and throwing out welcome heat.

'Aren't you cold, Jake?'

He didn't answer. He continued to build up the fire.

After a while her shivering subsided. She told Jake she needed the toilet but in fact she had an overwhelming desire to check her pregnancy status again. She was terrified that the shock to her system might make her lose her baby. She had hidden her supply of tester kits in places all round the hotel. There were some behind the reception desk, so, wrapped in her duvet, she went and collected one and took it into the toilet, locking the door behind her.

She unwrapped the stick, took down her pants and held the stick under her and urinated on it. She waited. Two thin but clear blue lines appeared. She knew it was too early to tell if the shock of fainting and falling had made her lose the baby, and that she would have to test again and again, but for now she was reassured.

This baby will be fine, she told herself. *This baby will be fine.*

She disposed of the stick, pulled up her pants and her jeans and went to wash her hands in the sink. The tap made a dyspeptic wheeze, but no water flowed. She tried another sink, turning on both taps, but without result. The water supply had stopped, or frozen. She could hear the airlock singing in the pipes from the opened tap. She put her ear to the mouth of the tap. The air in the pipe sounded so much like music, she had to strain her powers of listening to convince herself that it *wasn't* music she could hear coming out of the taps. And then after all she became certain that it was not an airlock she could hear but music after all, faint music being carried through the pipes. The music was orchestral, rising and falling; and then it was just the sound of an airlock again.

She opened the door of the bathroom and walked straight into Jake.

'Oh?'

'You okay? You were gone a long time.'

'Yes, I'm fine.'

'Everything okay?'

'Yes. Everything.'

He eyed her strangely. 'Let's get you back by the fire.'

Jake put his arm around her and tried to stroke some warmth into her as he led her back to the fireplace. He made a bed for her there and banked up the fire, complaining about how rapidly the logs burned before they had to be replenished. Zoe huddled as near to the fire as she could without actually setting her duvet aflame.

She told him about the water. 'Maybe it's frozen.'

'Maybe the generators in the village have just stopped pumping it. Don't worry about it. We'll drink red wine.'

Jake was already drinking red wine. No matter how much he downed, he didn't seem to get drunk. Zoe was not so sure. Previously she had happily joined him in sampling the best bottles, but now she was much more cautious. Too many strange things were happening and she wanted to keep a straight head. Plus there was her baby to think about, even in this world.

She hid her anxiety. When Jake was at her side she made a determined effort to keep things light; but when he went away for a few minutes, perhaps to fetch another bottle of wine, she got up and went to the glass doors of the reception, trying to peer through the mist, looking for movement.

And she saw it. Or if not movement, then in the form of more dark grey shapes. The mist billowed and drifted and she saw them again. The men. But now they were six. All in the same place as before. All gazing steadily back at the hotel, and smoking, smoking, smoking.

'Come quickly,' she said to Jake when he returned with a bottle of fine Bordeaux. 'But keep out of sight.'

He came up behind her, holding her, looking over her shoulder. She pointed a finger at the vague outline of the six men, all of them waiting like crows or patient birds of prey, watching the hotel.

'What is it?'

'Six of them. Now there are six.'

'Where?'

'Surely you can see them, Jake! Surely you can see their shape in the mist!'

'I don't see anything. Where are you looking?'

'There! And there! And there!'

Jake squinted into the mist. He shook his head minimally. He creased his forehead.

'Jake, tell me you can see six grey shapes! Just over there!'

Jake turned her to face him. 'I think you've been hallucinating stuff.'

'Look! Look! That's not a hallucination! They are all smoking cigarettes, staring back at us! You've seen the cigarette ends – that's where they're coming from!'

'I've seen the fag-ends, my darling, but I can't see anything or anyone. There's nothing there. Look, I'll go outside and check if it'll make you feel any better.'

'Don't you dare go out there!'

'Okay, okay, be calm. We'll stay here.'

Jake settled her by the fire again but not without her darting looks across her shoulder at the mist – and the grey figures she perceived outside. He sat with her, holding her cold hands, watching her, searching her face for external signs of internal distress.

Then he said, 'Do we still have two blue lines?'

'What?'

He nodded.

'You know?'

'Of course I know.'

She vented a huge sigh and hugged her midriff.

'Did you think,' he said, 'you could keep that a secret

from me? In this place, where nothing else is happening but you and me?' He was smiling.

'You're not angry?'

'Never. I was just waiting for you to tell me yourself that you were carrying our baby.' He looked at her with eyes full of anger and pity and desperate love. He took her hand and kissed it. It was a while before they spoke.

'How did you know?'

'I think you've got about a gross of those kits hidden in the room alone.'

'Right. Maybe I wanted you to find them. I've been testing several times a day. Sometimes hourly. I want it to change. And I don't want it to change. Would you have been happy, if it had been before? Before all this?'

'Given how I feel now? Yes I would. It would have been ecstasy.'

'And now?'

'I've been watching you carefully, knowing that you're carrying our baby. I don't mind telling you I've been worried.'

'About the baby?'

'Yes. And about the mother. You get cold; I don't. You get hungry; I don't. You get frightened by everything; I don't.'

She flicked an involuntary glance towards the glass doors. 'You mean to say you're not afraid? Not afraid of what's out there?'

He shook his head, no.

'That can't be true,' she said. 'I saw you take the axe with you when you went outside.'

'That was to reassure you, not me.'

'Why aren't you afraid, Jake? This place terrifies me.

I want to know what's going to happen to us; to our baby.'

'I can't explain why I'm not scared. I only know that my job is to look after you.'

'What's going to happen to our baby? What's going to happen?'

Jake sighed. It was the sigh of one who has no answer. He opened his mouth as if to speak and then changed his mind. Then he framed his lips into an O as if about to try again. But he was interrupted. Zoe's mobile phone rang.

It was ringing from her coat pocket, which she was wearing under her duvet. She almost ripped it from her pocket.

Jake took it from her. 'Let me answer it.'

He pressed the answer button and held the cellphone to his ear. He remained expressionless. He said nothing. Then he clicked off the phone and handed it back to her.

'Who was it? What did they say?'

'Same as before.'

'Did the voice say *la zone*? Is that what it said? The zone?'

'It was hard to make out, but I don't think he said *la zone* at all. He said *laissez sonner*. Which means *let it ring*. *Laissez sonner*. Then it went dead.'

'He wants me to let it ring?'

'That's what he said.'

'Why would he say that? *Laissez sonner*. Why would he tell you to let it ring?'

'I've no idea.' Jake checked the battery level. 'There's not much charge left in this. But I think we should put it aside and if it rings, we just leave it.'

'Why?'

'Because that's what he said.'

'But how do you know that's a good thing? How do you know that it's not someone who wants to harm us? Maybe by answering it we're keeping him away. Have you thought of that?'

'No one is going to harm us.'

'You can't say that. You don't know!'

'We're in a place beyond harm.'

Zoe clasped her belly. 'I wish I could believe that. But I don't. Who is calling us? Who are those men out there?'

'You're feverish. Come on; keep warm.' He threw another couple of logs on the fire. 'Damn these logs! They don't last five minutes!'

Jake got up and set Zoe's mobile phone on the reception desk. Then he sat down beside her again, and they watched the phone, from that short distance, as if it might perform an act of combustion, like indoor fireworks.

It didn't ring.

Her teeth were chattering again. She was feverish, but it was a cold fever; she just couldn't get warm. Jake piled her with covers and stoked the fire and while his back was turned she looked over at the window.

There it was again, a face. A scarf masking the lower half. Darting eyes, the hint of red lips above the scarf. The eyes were like pinpoints of fire, grains of light; those half-hidden lips were moving, forming unheard words.

She was on the point of warning Jake when the window itself shattered, and glass crystals rained into the room. The pressure within the lobby escaped into the dark and a wind from outside roared and shrieked, driving a blast of cold air around the room, gusting at the fire, threatening to blow out the flames. The wind shrieked and the mist roiled in at the broken window like wraiths liberated, baleful, mischievous, searching.

Jake leapt to his feet and grabbed a mattress. He dragged it to the window, ramming it hard into the aperture, stuffing it until it filled the hole, muffling the shrieking wind.

She was shivering now, too violently to speak, to tell him what she had seen at the window before the glass blew in.

He said, 'I'm going to get you some cognac.'

Even though she knew he was only gone for perhaps a minute, two minutes at most, in that time she saw the light outside fading, incrementally, as if visibility were being shut down by precise mathematical commands. In those few moments the logs on the fire flared, burned, split, fell apart and died down.

Jake returned with the cognac. Before he gave it to her he lit two candles and set them nearby. Then he poured a glass of cognac apiece. She sipped it. He did too, but complained it tasted of nothing. 'According to the price list we could never afford this. You're going to have to remember it for me.'

'What happened to the window, Jake?'

'Remember it for me.'

'How can I remember cognac?'

'Approximate.'

She took a sip. 'Our first kiss. You were a little drunk.'

He savoured more of the cognac, without taking his eyes from her. 'I love you, Zoe. Never abandon something so deep.'

'What?'

'What's what?'

'What you just said to me. Never abandon something so deep.'

'I said that?'

'Yes.'

'I don't remember. It's getting so I can't remember what I said to you two seconds ago. Look at the fire. I feel like I only put those logs on a few minutes ago and they've burned down.'

'You did.'

'And look at the candles.' He nodded at the yellow, flickering flame. The candle was burning fast, so fast it was possible to see the candle shrinking as the molten wax rolled back from the burning wick.

'What's happening, Jake?'

'Time seems to have … Our precious time will … I don't know, my darling, I can't even think to the end of a sentence. Isn't that funny?'

'I'm very frightened.'

He turned away from her and threw some more logs on the fire. They flared quickly. Twilight had already turned to darkness outside. She lay back on her bed and felt herself dozing. So exhausted was she that she gave in to it.

She was awoken by what she took to be a wolf howling in the mountains. The air was freezing on her cheeks and a stiff breeze lifted her hair. The animal's howl came again: a sustained ululation travelling clear, mournful, melancholy and yet oddly sweet in the cold night air. She sat up to look out of the window and to her astonishment the window was gone.

Not only was the window gone, but so too had the glass doors. Two complete walls of the hotel had been removed while she slept. She cast about her, trying to make sense of it.

Two walls still sheltered her as before, but only two walls; the fire burned brightly in one of them, the logs sparking merrily, flames flaring and twisting in the grate. But the entire south side of the hotel, along with the eastern wall, had gone, though the roof above her remained. Now she looked out directly onto the slope of the mountain, with its terrifying expanse of gleaming moonlit-white, like the wing or shoulder of a primordial spirit of nature.

Jake was in the act of lighting another candle. He smiled at her. A breeze chased around the sheltered quarter and he held his hand across the flame to stop it from guttering. Even as it guttered she could see the flame was burning down fast – faster than a candle should burn, faster than was sensible.

Another howl came back across the open eastern expanse of snow, within which she could no longer see any shape or form of the village. But in the darkness for a moment she thought she could see the twin red points of the animal's eyes reflecting back at her; then she saw more tiny red embers. One of the embers flared briefly and died down. Then another. She realised it was not eyes, but the lighted cigarettes of the smoking men. They had moved nearer to the open walls of the hotel. Two of them had dropped to a crouch, their fingers grazing the snow in front of them. One was pointing at the fireplace. The others cast glances at the ceiling.

'It's the men!' she told Jake. 'They're just outside.'

'Where?' he said.

'There! Look at the lights! The tiny lights.'

He looked casually out into the darkness, scanning the wax-like wastes of unforgiving snow. 'Yes,' he said. 'I see them. I'll go and speak with them.' But something in his voice betrayed the fact that he couldn't see them at all, that he was simply humouring her.

'No!' she cried in horror. 'You must never do that. Stay here. Stay.'

'That's right. You stay here,' he said soothingly, his voice oddly tranquil, no more than a murmur. 'Stay here.'

He got up and walked out of their sheltered corner. This time he didn't even take the axe. She hauled herself to her feet to watch, almost hyperventilating as Jake walked across the snow towards the men. He seemed no more than a silhouette creeping in the snow. He drew within a few metres of the men before he squatted down on his haunches.

The men began talking and making animated gestures with their hands. She couldn't hear any of it. Though she strained to catch what they were saying, their talk was obliterated by the wind buffeting at the remaining walls of the hotel. There was also something amiss with the way in which Jake engaged with the men. He was not looking at them. He was not even facing them. He talked, and nodded or shook his head occasionally as if in some kind of negotiation, but it was as if they were in different worlds; and as if he couldn't see them, nor they him.

This curious negotiation went on for a long time, during which the candles burned down to their stumps and the fire died.

When Jake came back, he looked grave. He didn't

answer any of her questions. He stoked the fire again and banked up the logs.

'What did the men say?' she demanded.

'The important thing,' he said, pulling the pile of duvets closer around her, 'is to keep you warm.'

'Do you know what they want?'

'Who?'

'The men! Did they say what they want?'

'Yes, they did. But it's hard for me to remember. Very hard.' He poured her another glass of cognac and refused to answer any more questions until she'd drunk it. Exasperated and exhausted, she gulped it and lay back again. Her weariness outweighed her fear, and she felt herself dozing again.

When she woke this time, the remaining walls and the ceiling of the hotel had been removed, along with the entire hotel lobby. There was still a fire, but it burned merrily on the snow itself, without the surround of the brick chimney or the mantelpiece or even the hearth. Jake was loading logs from a diminished pile onto the fire and they were burning supernaturally quickly.

'All the candles are gone,' he said with a sheepish grin, like a man trying to make light of a difficult situation.

She sat up immediately and looked for signs of the men – telltale burning embers in the dark, movement of any kind. There was none. She looked up at the open sky. The stars were locked in a frozen cascade, twinkling in their billion-fold, an army of semi-immortal deities. She gasped, her breath congealing in the icy air.

Then there was that howl again, followed by three crisp barks, and as she looked across the snow she saw a dog running towards them. Jake scrambled to his feet. 'It's Sadie!' he cried. 'She's come back!'

The dog bulleted towards Jake and he ran to meet her. Sadie leapt up to greet him, tail thrashing, whimpering, licking his face. They rolled together in the snow. 'It's Sadie,' Jake called to Zoe. 'Can you believe she came back?'

Zoe watched as the dog's enthusiasm quietened. Jake sat on the snow as she snuffled in his ear. It almost seemed to Zoe that the two of them were having a conversation. Sadie stretched her neck and pointed her moist snout at the moon as Jake scratched her between the ears. She snuffled in his ear again.

He stopped stroking her and became still.

The dog snuffled in his ear a third time. Jake's head fell forwards. He became still, his hand placed flat on Sadie's flank. They stayed that way for some time and Zoe thought something must be wrong, but after a while Jake became reanimated, stroking the dog's flank and tickling the sweet spot behind her ears. Eventually he got up and led the dog over to Zoe.

Sadie came and flung herself flat on the snow next to Zoe. But when she looked up at Jake, his face was wet with tears.

'What is it?'

He shook his head, then lowered himself beside Zoe and hugged her and kissed her neck.

'Jake?'

'Sadie explained it all to me.'

'It?'

'Yes. She told me everything.'

'What did she tell you?'

'Well, she's a dog and of course she can't explain

everything but somehow she made me understand some things. And I'm going to tell you, but it's going to make me cry, my darling.'

She held his face in her hands. Fat tears, snow-reflecting crystals, were already streaking his face. Sadie, wagging her tail, shuffled up to him and licked away his tears. He laughed, stroking her.

'You see, we cheated death.'

'We did?'

'Yes.'

'Does that mean we're safe?'

'We were always safe. But we cheated death, and because we couldn't let each other go we found some extra time.'

'No.'

'Yes. We found some extra time. The dream of the present moment was interrupted for us. We're watching all of this through the seams between life and death.'

'What are you saying?'

'Our love. It gave us extra time. It cheated death.'

'But that's a good thing. Isn't it? Isn't that a good thing, Jake?'

'Yes. Yes it is.'

There came from somewhere in the mountains a tiny shivering sound, faint and distant, at that moment almost indiscernible, but though they didn't know it yet, they both surely heard it.

'No,' she said, shaking her head. 'No. I don't think I like what you're saying.'

'Because you know what's coming?'

'No.'

'Yes. It's because you know what's coming. Listen to that.'

A steady, rhythmic rattle, like crushed ice shaken in a cocktail glass, or perhaps like the wheezing of an old steam train climbing a gradient, sounded out of the far distance.

'What's that, Jake?'

'You know what it is.'

'No. I don't. I don't want to know.'

'Don't worry, it's all good. It's all good.'

'How can it be good?'

'I'm keeping you here. I thought I was keeping you warm, but I've been keeping you here. Our love. Keeping us.'

'We'll be all right here. We've done fine so far. The baby.'

'No. It's already passing. We cheated death, but just for a little while.'

The rhythmic rattle, a kind of hissing in the sharp, cold air, was drawing closer. And then she recognised the sound.

'You're abandoning me, Jake? You're leaving me here?'

'Listen to me. Everything we are we have built from everything we have done together. If we drank a glass of wine and we said it tasted like this or that, then that's how it tasted. One has to help remember it for the other.'

The sound was growing now and was accompanied by a kind of drumming in the earth, under the snow. The drumming was the sound of hooves and the rattle was the shiver of harness bells.

'No. Please don't leave me here.'

'Everything, our whole lives, has been a series of delights and griefs that are gone for ever; gone unless we remember them for each other.'

The shiver of the harness bells was louder now, and the great black horse they adorned appeared out of the dark, its vast sweating flanks gleaming, its breath rising and billowing in the freezing air, its huge red plume, red like wine caught in a jewelled cup or like blood in a silver chalice, shaking before it and cutting a swathe through the brittle air.

'You can't abandon me on the snow! You're not going to. You're not.'

'I'm top banana today, my darlin' girl, and there's only a seat for one of us.'

'No. I'm not having it, Jake.'

'All you have to do is refuse to forget.'

She grabbed at his lapels and hung on to him with a ferocious grip. 'This is not going to happen.'

'You know how to do that, don't you, Zoe? You know how to refuse to forget?' He floated his index finger over her gripping arms and touched her lightly in the middle of her forehead. 'You just keep this eye open. And you'll see me everywhere. Just everywhere.'

He pulled away from her.

The giant black horse and sledge approached at pace, taking a track that curved away from them both. Jake turned and started taking long, purposeful strides towards the horse, aiming to intercept its path.

'Jake!' she screamed and scrambled to her feet, stunned, incredulous to see him walking away from her.

But it didn't stop him. He proceeded on his steady determined way across the snow. Already the horse was slowing as it made the slope. Jake had already covered a few paces before Zoe set off after him, running. But she had no strength. Jake was heading to intercept the horse, but even though he was only walking steadily towards it and she was running, it was Zoe who was falling back. She ran faster, but the irrational distance between them only increased instead of shortened. She fell and got up again, running, slipping on the snow, her feet going from under her.

For a moment it seemed that Jake might not catch the horse; but then as he approached the animal and the awe-inspiring vapours rising from its flanks, it seemed to slow deliberately, to break its trot to a brisk walk; and in that break Jake marched up to the sledge, finding a step up onto the footboard, and from there he scrambled into the safe pocket of the black leather upholstery. The horse tossed its head and recovered its trot again, picking up speed as it found a flat track.

Still Zoe ran after them, screaming at Jake, trying to make pace. For a moment she even drew abreast of the giant sledge, reaching as she ran, but the footboard seemed to climb away from her as she scrambled alongside, and the door to the carriage loomed above her outstretched fingers. The sledge seemed to swell in size until the footboard was well out of reach, or until she was impossibly small. She fell on her knees in the snow, crying after Jake.

Sadie, keeping pace with the sledge, stopped and stole a look back at her. Then the dog bulleted across the snow to follow her master, quickly catching up with the sledge before both it and the horse disappeared into the swirling darkness.

16

Zoe was numb with shock and cold. It had never occurred to her that Jake would abandon her. As she looked around her she could see nothing but a wide expanse of snow with the mountain slope on one side and dark pools of pine trees on the other. The town, and whatever comforts or resources it had previously offered, had gone. She understood that she was alone in this place, and pregnant.

She retreated to the flickering embers of the fire, but it only served to remind her how bone-numbingly cold she was. There were only a half-dozen or so logs remaining, the very last of the supply. She picked up one of the logs but it felt light and insubstantial in her hands, and when she put it onto the embers it flared and caught unnaturally. She huddled over the flame, feeling weak, drawing the duvet around her shoulders, shuddering with the pain of a cold that scraped crystal fingers across her beating heart.

She stared up at the stars in the winter sky. They had never in her life looked so multiple, so incalculable. The stars did not look down upon her. They seemed almost to turn away, with disinterested hard energy.

The log burning on the fire split and fell apart. She put another two on the flame and watched them burn rapidly. Time was racing, hunting for its correct velocity.

The logs burned out like wads of paper. She put the very last of the wood on the fire, almost with a dedication to find out what would happen in this fleeting existence when they were all gone, when all resources were gone. She knew she could not survive this cold. She stroked her belly and watched the logs burn.

Death would come; a real death, oblivion. But she wondered if even that could take away the sting of loneliness she felt from Jake's betrayal.

She sensed her mind closing down as the last log turned to embers. But then she saw them. Figures coming towards her out of the snow. Shapes, shadows, approaching her. They were roughly human, no more than silhouettes against the star-lit snow. Some of them had trumpets. One put his mouth to the trumpet and gave a long, low blast. Others had silver whistles and began to blow on them. More trumpets sounded. They were circling, moving in towards her.

So this was how she was to be taken. Perhaps they were demons coming for her. Amid the trumpets and the whistle-blowing she heard them shouting until they were all raising their voices. They were closing in.

These beings were led by the figures she had seen waiting outside the hotel. Men in black garb, their mouths partially wound in scarves. The smoking men. They were still smoking now. It was as if they had waited for the last embers of the last log to burn out before they began to throw down their cigarettes and approach her.

She had no strength to resist as they reached out for her, clawing at her. A sleepy paralysis took her over. If she was to be carried off to hell in this way she had no fight left. She thought only of Jake, and of the baby growing inside her.

17

I am a long way down. And yet I see it from above. White drifts of six-pointed crystals of tender, tender snow. The crystals interlock and make a wall. If I can get through the wall. If I can get through.

Then the crystals change and start to run past my eyes like complex machine code on a grey computer screen. No, it's DNA. Strings of DNA running by, swimming by. No, it's complex mathematical formulae, tiny numerals spinning before my eyes. Now it's white cotton seed borne by a breeze, but in incredible slo-mo. It's a tiny current, an eddy in Time. There: it's snowflakes again.

Just snowflakes.

The snowflakes are in my ears, in my mouth, in my nose, like cocaine. I tried it once. You can keep it for your mother: it's not a patch on where being in love can get you. The blood in my veins is frozen but it sings of love.

I can hear the sword of an angel scything through the air. *Whop, whop, whop.* Oh come. I can feel the vibration in the earth, the disturbance of air currents, the icy terror in the blade, the vestigial fire in my blood.

It's very nice. I can let go.

I can fall into a place thronged with people. Their voices are a pleasing babble, and the air from their many mouths rises and cushions me as I fall gently among them. Many people come and go. I recognise some of them. There are two women standing by the desk. I somehow know them. I know their language. I know what they are talking about. A man walks by me and winks. Trying it on. I smell his cologne. Three uniformed women work behind a broad desk, busy dealing with people. One is young, with her hair scraped back and tied in a pretty ponytail. She presses a phone to her ear. Her older colleague has hair the colour of fire. She wears black-framed spectacles. She is processing a credit card. Another colleague talks to a man in a grey suit, struggling to hear what he has to say because the place is loud with excited chatter. People wait in a line by the desk, checking in, checking out.

I see the concierge, in his smart maroon and grey livery. He sees me and raises his eyebrows at me. He waves. I seem to recognise him. He waves at me again, beckoning me forwards across the busy lobby. But I can't move. The concierge whispers something to another man before he picks up an envelope from his blond-wood desk. 'Madam!' he says to me. 'Madam!' He waves the envelope at me.

It's not for me, I want to say.

I am afraid of the concierge. His bald head is illuminated by the strong lights overhead. There is a bloom of sweat on his shiny brow. He makes his way towards me through the people thronging the lobby. 'Madam!' he says again.

I pluck up courage and in a clear voice I say, 'But it's not for me.'

'But madam,' says the concierge, closing in on me with a smile, placing the envelope in my hand, 'it is indeed for you, madam.' He stands there, the sweet smile still upon his lips, as if waiting for me to open the envelope.

I am afraid to open it. But with trembling fingers I tear it open and I reach inside. But there is nothing. Or not exactly nothing, but what there is is nothing more than a card. It is a kind of Tarot card, but not like any Tarot card I know. It depicts a tree. The words at the bottom say '*L'arbre de Vie*'. Tree of life, I know. But it is not like any tree of life I have seen. It is more like a Christmas tree, decorated with curious objects and impossible fruit.

I look up at the concierge because I want to say, 'What does this mean?' But the concierge has gone. All of them, everyone, everything. All are gone.

Zoe opened her eyes to a white expanse. She felt the silk and honey of warmth in her veins. An odour of disinfectant. A brightly illuminated room. The white expanse was that of cotton sheets and a pillowcase.

There was a nurse looking at her. They blinked at each other. The nurse walked away quickly and returned within seconds with another woman, this one in a doctor's white coat.

The woman bent over her. 'Zoe?' she said.

'Yes.'

'You know what happened?' She spoke with a strong French accent.

'Avalanche.'

'Yes.'

'My husband?'

The doctor sat on the bed and took her hand. 'We didn't find him yet. We only got you just in time. I'm so sorry.'

Zoe tilted back her head and opened her mouth in a silent wail and let the bitter salt tears flow over her face. The doctor waited patiently for the sobbing and convulsions to subside. But they didn't. She said some words to the nurse in French and the nurse produced a medical syringe which she handed to the doctor.

'No,' Zoe said, 'no. I don't want to go back to sleep. I don't want that.'

The doctor nodded. She put the syringe into a dish. 'As you wish. If you want it, you tell me.'

Zoe looked around her at the room. Both the doctor and the nurse stared at her, as if they were waiting for her to say something.

'You might not think this,' the doctor said, 'but you have been very lucky. Very lucky. You were at the door of death. Do you know that you are pregnant?'

Zoe nodded.

'The baby seems to be fine,' the doctor said. 'We'll watch that.'

Zoe felt choked. Huge sobs were trying to fight their way out of her, but she pushed them down.

'How do you feel? I mean, physically?'

Zoe shook her head. Her grief was physical.

'Apart from a few bruises I didn't find anything,' the doctor said. 'This bloodshot in your eyes will go after a while. It's from the pressure of the snow, weighing on you.'

She struggled to speak. 'Can I see?'

The doctor asked the nurse to find her a mirror.

Zoe held up the mirror. The whites of her eyes had indeed been turned all red. It was the way Jake had looked.

'It will pass. You just need to rest. You have a lot of things to think about.' The doctor stood up. 'Look, there's a man outside. He's the one who found you. He dug you out of the snow. He would like to speak with you and he's been waiting outside since you were brought in. But if you're not up to it I can send him away. He can come back later.'

'No, please let him come in.'

The doctor nodded to the nurse, who went out of the room. After a few minutes she returned with an elderly gentleman, his leathery, tanned face wreathed with lines. His grey hair was shaved close to his skull. He had a miraculously thin and close-trimmed moustache. There was a smile on his lips but his eyes glittered with sympathy for her grief, like sunlight on frost.

It was perfectly natural that Zoe should hold out her arms to embrace the stranger who had saved her. The doctor drew back so that he could lean across the bed and accept her embrace. '*Vous bénisse! Vous bénisse!*' he said.

He reeked of tobacco.

'Thank you thank you thank you.'

He stood back and spoke to her in French, not appearing to care if Zoe could understand. The doctor translated. 'He says you are the third person he has dug out of the snow, but you were the one he had the least hope for.'

'Can you ask him how long I was under the snow?'

'He says maybe twenty minutes, maybe more. Your holiday rep had seen you go up early and she was able to give the rescue team your number. They were nearby and they got there very fast. But all the others were looking in the wrong place. He says he listened to the snow.'

'Listened?'

'That's what he said. He said his colleagues were using thermal sensor equipment but they were wrong. He went to a different place and found you. He said they quickly got hold of your phone number and tried to call. He says he heard your phone ringing under the snow. But it kept stopping and he was praying to let it ring.'

'*Laissez sonner.*'

'*Oui. Laissez sonner,*' said the old man.

She knew his voice. But it wasn't possible that, buried under snow, she could have answered her phone.

Then he handed her a card. It was wet, almost disintegrating, and it was the size of a large playing card. On one side was a picture of a Christmas tree, decorated with gifts. She had seen it before. But this time there were no words on the card.

'What's this?'

The man spoke and the doctor translated. 'He said it was in your fist.'

The man spoke again to the doctor, flicking at his own large ears and smiling at Zoe. 'He says he's always had good hearing. His friends joke about it. And he said he heard tiny movements under the snow. A tiny scratching. Then he knew you were there, and he called the rest of them. And they all came.'

'What did he ... ?' she tried.

'He doesn't trust the new ways. He said he even gave you cognac when he found you, though it's forbidden now.'

'I remember the taste of the cognac.'

The doctor translated and the old man's eyebrows danced. He spoke in animated fashion. Then the man became sombre and turned to look at the doctor.

'Now he says he doesn't want to look at you while he apologises for not finding the other one.'

Despite this, the old man turned and nodded at her.

'Please tell him that he did save another one. He did.'

The doctor explained something to the old man. He

stepped over to the bed and tenderly he reached out a weathered hand and placed it on the cotton covers above her belly. He let his hand rest there for a moment and again the reek of his tobacco was strong.

'He's very happy,' the doctor said. 'He's a coffin-maker in the village, and he says he's glad to be involved with life instead of death.'

Zoe felt the tears welling up. The man wished her luck and took his leave.

Once more the doctor offered her something that would help her to sleep. Zoe refused it. There would be a great deal to think about in the coming days, and a lot to do. She lay back with her hand resting on her midriff. She wondered if Jake had made a deal in some dark place; a trade wherein he had not abandoned her at all, but had saved her; and if such a thing were possible.

She heard a light grazing on the window and she looked up to see huge, gentle six-pointed flakes from a picture book blown by a breeze onto the glass. It was snowing again.

ACKNOWLEDGEMENTS

For long-term support and friendship: Anne Williams, Pete Williams, Simon Spanton, Luigi Bonomi, Pete Coleborn, Julie-Anne Hudson, Brig Eaton, Chris Fowler, Julie Flanders, Daniel Hanson, Julie Hanson, Helen and Tim Bennet. Thanks and praise also to Lisa Rogers for superb copy-editing. Finally, to the memory of the inspirational Robert Holdstock.